HE BRINGS OUT THE HOOD IN ME

NIKKI BROWN

Created with Vellum

FOLLOW ME ON SOCIAL MEDIA

Thank you all for your continued support, it's definitely appreciated!

Facebook: Author Nikki Brown
Facebook Reading Group: Nikki's Haven ♥
Instagram: @nikkibrown_theauthor
Twitter: @NikkiBrownSWP
www.nikkibrownwrites.com

Text Nikki to 66866 to join my mailing list

ALSO BY NIKKI BROWN

Messiah and Reign 1-3

I Won't Play A Fool For You (Messiah and Reign spinoff)

My Love And His Loyalty 1-3

I Deserve your love 1-3

Bury My Heart 1-2

Beautiful Mistake 1-3

Beautiful Revenge

Riding Hard For A Thug 1-3

You're The Cure To The Pain He Caused

Key To The Heart Of A Boss 1-3

I Got Love For A Carolina Hustla 1-3

A Hood Love Like No Other 1-2

Vexed: The Streets Never Loved Me 1-2

Hood Witches

Trap 4 Lyfe: Down To Ride For A Carolina Menace 1-2

Hood Witches Need Love Too

He Brings Out The Hood In Me

CHAPTER ONE

S*etback*

"I shouldn't have to ask my dad for shit Trouble, I had the got damn money!" Sutton yelled in her fiancé's face. She was really having a hard time not hitting him in the face, she was so pissed that she couldn't contain herself. Her hands shook lightly while she held them in closed fists down by her side.

Trouble had yet again gambled all of their money away. She would have never known had the bank not called about the late payment. They were supposed to catch up on their mortgage before the bank took possession of the house, but it looked like that wouldn't happen and it was all thanks to Trouble.

Sutton had options, but she didn't feel the need to exercise them because she made plenty of money to pay her bills and still be able to live a nice lifestyle. Her only downfall was Trouble and she knew it. She also knew that if she ended up having to call her father that she would never hear the end of it, and she didn't want to do that.

"A nigga was up Sut, you know how I get when I'm up. I lost sight of the big picture and fucked up. I know you gone forgive a nigga. Just let me go win that shit back. Let me get some money out of your business account."

Sutton's eyes stretched wide as she looked at him like he was stupid. She knew that he was in deep, but she didn't know that it was this big of a problem. Even though he had pretty much gambled away their entire savings, she still had hope that he would turn it around. Looks like she was the stupid one.

Sutton broke out into a full-blown laugh, she grabbed her stomach and folded over. To keep from going to jail the only thing she could do was laugh. She wasn't sure what kind of drugs Trouble was on at the moment, but he clearly wasn't thinking straight if he thought that she was about to dip into her business account for any reason.

She owned a hair salon that her father got her when she was straight out of school. It was her mother's insurance policy that her dad saved just for her that bought the building, so it meant a lot to her. That was the only thing that she had to remind her of her mother.

Sutton's mother and father were deep in the drug game for the majority of her life, so she was spoiled and used to having everything and everyone at her beck and call. It wasn't until her mother was assassinated at a drug deal gone bad that her dad decided to hang up his dealer days and go legit with his life and his freedom. Her dad never got over the loss of his wife and neither had Sutton, but the two had each other and that tragedy brought them closer together. She was daddy's little girl and they were each other's everything.

"Yeah, no thanks. If I dip into my business account for anything it will be to clean up your fuck up, but it damn sure won't be to add to it." Sutton rolled her eyes long and hard before she walked away shaking her head. "Plus, my father is linked to that account and you don't want them problems," she said with her back still to him.

"Yo I'm tired of you talking to me like a little fucking kid!" Trouble yelled at her back.

He knew that he had fucked up once again, but it was no reason for her to speak to him that way. She was his woman and she was supposed to have his back; good, bad, or indifferent. It was like she always found a way to throw her father in his face and he hated it.

When they first met, she knew that he was into gambling. At that time, he was on top and making so much money that he didn't know what to do with it, so it wasn't an issue. That didn't last long at all, it seemed like when he got with her, she became his bad luck charm. The losing became more frequent than the winning, and that's where the issues came in. Sutton blamed herself for what was going on in their relationship because as long as he was winning, she condoned it, but the consequences were starting to eat her up.

Since Sutton was making her own money, had a career, and a company, Trouble felt like he had something to prove to her. Almost like they were in competition. Trouble started getting greedy with the gambling and stopped being smart, so he started to lose instead of win, and he blamed her for it. If she hadn't been so got damn independent, he wouldn't fuck up the way that he did.

Trouble came from a line of fuck ups; his dad was an old thief who got killed trying to rip off the wrong drug dealer and his mom was a scam artist who was in jail doing a five-year bid for check fraud. There wasn't a person in his family that was on top of their game and he was no better.

Hudson, Sutton's father knew that Trouble was nothing but trouble the minute that his daughter introduced them. He couldn't for the life of him understand why his daughter made such bad decisions in men, he showed her at a young age how a man should treat her, and it was like she searched for the exact opposite of that. Hudson made sure his daughter never wanted for a thing. So, he chopped it up as her just being defiant, he loved her anyway, but he kept his distance. His only no no was for her to date a drug dealer with fear that she would end up like her mother. He blamed himself for that daily.

"Trouble you are more than welcomed to leave." Sutton shrugged her shoulders. "I'm not forcing you to be here."

Sutton loved Trouble, which was why she agreed to marry him, but his up and down gambling debt was starting to be too much, and she refused to let someone bring her down.

She was starting to see just how his gambling was affecting her and how she was able to move.

"So, it's like that?" Trouble's long strides caught up to Sutton before she could move out of the way.

"You're making it this way, I'm supposed to be safe with you, I don't feel safe. I never know when your gambling debt is gonna blow up in *our* face. You're already blowing the mortgage, what else you gonna do? Hell, you gone sell me next?" He sighed heavily and took a step back creating a little distance between the two of them.

"I told you that I'm gonna fix it I just need some cushion," he pleaded with her. All he needed was a hot G and he could go back to the underground casino and get his money back plus some. He just needed her to help him.

"Well you gone have to find another way to get that cushion because I can't help you." Sutton crossed her arms across her chest and stared at Trouble in his eyes. It was love there she could feel it; the attraction was still there because her nipples hardened every time she took in his tall lean frame. It was just that the trouble that surrounded Trouble was starting to be too much for her.

Trouble was very easy on the eyes, standing a little over six feet. His slender athletic frame housed simple yet defined muscles in his arms and chest area. You could get lost in his big brown eyes, he liked to use them to his advantage especially when he knew he was in the wrong.

Nothing beat those thick lips of his that he knew exactly what to do with. That was one of the main reasons that it was so hard for Sutton to walk away. Their sex life was amazing, that and the fact that she really wanted to spend her life with him, or so she thought.

"Aight, after this come up don't be sitting somewhere with your hand out. Remember this conversation."

"As long as you handle your part of the bills then we good play boy." Sutton smiled and walked the rest of the way in the room. She had made plans to go to some party with her best friend Piper and after her fight with Trouble, she needed it.

She had met some dude that she was head over heels for already and she wanted to go and check up on him at some party that his cousin was throwing but she didn't want to go alone. Being her best friend, Sutton knew that she couldn't let her go alone, she knew exactly how she could be. Sutton was a hot head, but Piper would get herself into the dumbest situations and fight her way out of them. The way she saw it they both had too much to lose.

Stepping into the shower Sutton pulled out her favorite Dove soap and began to wash the stress of the current events away. All she wanted to do was do hair and make her mom proud, but Trouble was making that hard for her. Shaking her head all she could think about was the ten grand that he had gambled away. *Damn I don't want to go into my business account.*

Her heart was beginning to harden with all of Trouble's bullshit. Granted, she knew that he was into the gambling scene when they got together but she just didn't know how deep or that she would get the burden of his debt.

All she knew was that he made lots of money and he was

able to do for her what her dad had done her whole life and that excited her. It excited her to the point that she ignored all of the signs, the ones that led her to the situation she was currently in.

"Can I join you?" before she could object Trouble was in the shower with her and all of her naked glory.

As bad as she wanted to tell him to get the fuck out, she couldn't. Sex with them was always amazing and Trouble knew that was the one way to wash away her attitude and possibly get the money he needed to pay his gambling debt before the Maler brothers came after him.

"Trouble sex won't fix everything." Sutton was so unsure of her words as she focused on Trouble's thick dick that was standing at attention and ready to invade the walls that it considered home, at least when he was at home.

"I know that, but I love you and I hate when we fight, I didn't want to leave this house with us pissed off at each other. Plus, he missed you." Trouble said thrusting his hips forward.

Tucking his lip between his teeth he looked down at Sutton who stood about 5'6", she was so pretty to him. Damn near perfect, and that very thing kept him around and kept him in his feelings at the same time. She was too perfect, he felt like he wasn't good enough for her and that's why he continuously fucked up, trying to prove otherwise and in his eyes that was her fault too.

Her light brown skin glowed under the shower light, and it made her honey colored eyes look lighter than they already were. Her doe shaped eyes were the one thing that drew him to her all those years ago, and they were also the very thing that made him feel less than a man when he looked into them.

Before she could respond, Trouble had her back against the wall and his dick entering her roughly, just the way she liked it. Throwing her head back, Sutton put all of the issues that they were dealing with in the back of her mind and allowed him to take her on a ride, a ride that she desperately needed.

"Ssssss yesssss baby," she moaned as he lifted her up and down his shaft. "God yessss."

"Still the best pussy I ever had." And he was telling the truth. No matter how many women Trouble slept with, he knew that none of them ever amounted to Sutton. "Damn baby I love you."

"You too Brax!" Sutton said calling Trouble by his government name. He loved when she did that and the way it rolled off of her tongue. "Fuck I'm gonna cum."

"Say that shit again baby, so I can cum with you," Trouble taunted.

"I'm gonna cum Braxton." She threw her head back and began matching him stroke for stroke. Trouble took the chance to attack her exposed neck while he had her where he wanted her. "Yes, baby shit."

"Fuck baby grip my shit just like that." Sutton's pussy had a massive hold on his dick, and he was about to lose it, he couldn't pull out if he wanted to. He knew that he needed to because Sutton had expressed on more than one occasion that she didn't want babies right now, not until she was where she wanted to be financially. "Fuck!"

Troubled yelled out one more time before he grunted and emptied his seeds inside of her womb. Sutton immediately became pissed, she was starting to think that Trouble did that shit on purpose. He knew how she felt about kids right now, but he still did dumb shit like this.

She was madder at herself because she should have made him strap up. Pushing against his chest for him to let her down, Trouble immediately sensed her attitude and went right into fixing mode. He knew that she would never agree to give him the money that he needed if they were fighting. He kicked himself for not being smarter about the situation.

"I'm sorry baby, the pussy was so good I couldn't pull out. You want me to go to the store to get you the morning after pill?"

She looked at him and shook her head. How could she keep putting herself in these dumb situations that her dad warned her about? It's not like she didn't know better, but here she was. Just the thought of having a baby with an habitual gambler turned her stomach, she needed to move smarter.

"No, it's okay, I'll pick one up when Piper comes and scoops me up." She pushed passed him into the stream of the water that was starting to get cold. Shaking her head, she had it in her mind that she was going to get fucked up tonight and party like her life depended on it. With all the bullshit that she had been going through with Trouble, she deserved a night of fun and that's exactly what she was going to do.

~

"A barn Piper? Really? You think I'm about to go throw my ass in a circle in a fucking barn? What if I dip it low and a snake crawl up and bite my coochie, then what bitch?" Sutton looked over at Piper who was now bent over laughing so hard she was snorting. "I don't see a damn thing funny bitch."

"Girl yo bougie ass need to get out more." Piper's laughs were drawing nasty looks from Sutton. Sutton could be a little extra at times but that was her girl and she knew how to bring her back to earth when need be. "It's a barn but trust me when I say it's nice as fuck in here, just chill and watch."

Reluctantly Sutton got out of the car and walked in the direction of the Barn. She could hear the music and cars were everywhere, so she let her guard down a little. *Chill bitch you need this, even if it is in a fucking barn,* she coached herself as Piper reached for the handle of the door. Sutton grabbed her arm.

"If this some bullshit, I'm leaving yo ass here and you can find your own way home." Glaring into Sutton's eyes, Piper tried to find the humor in her words. When she didn't find any, she giggled and made her way inside.

The big chandelier in the middle of the barn that hung down over the middle of the makeshift dance floor took

Suttons words and shoved them down her throat. The fancy tables that lined the room and glass bar to her right had her eating every word she said prior.

Women were dressed in the least amount of clothes that they could find, and the men were damn near fucking them on the dance floor. There was definitely money in the building, and it was in abundance. Sutton still couldn't believe that a barn could look like this in the inside. She was expecting hay and horse shit, boy was she wrong.

"Damn, it's some fucking ballers in here." Piper said sticking her hand in the back pocket of her tight skinny leg jeans that she opted to wear, showing off her thick thighs and wide hips. A slight breeze came through brushing across her exposed belly button causing her to giggle.

"So where is this man we came to see?" Sutton said taking a look around the building.

Her eyes met the sexiest, darkest and most mysterious pair of eyes that she had ever seen on a man. They were so dark it was almost scary. A cold chill ran down the back of her neck even though it was damn near 70 degrees out. Her nipples hardened immediately as she forced herself to tear her eyes away from the sexy gentlemen.

"There he is with some skinny bitch bent over the chair," Piper said taking off in the direction of that action before she could get the words out of her mouth. Sutton sighed and headed in the direction Piper took off in.

"I did not come here to be fighting," Sutton said looking down at the all red Louis she decided to finally wear. Her dad had got them for her for her birthday this year and she had yet to take them out of the box until now. She was gonna be pissed if Piper started some shit and caused her to fuck them up or worse, lose one.

"Menz what the fuck nigga!" Piper yelled out gaining the attention of the other people in the barn. "How in the fuck you gone invite me here and then be doing this shit?" Piper seemed genuinely hurt and Sutton couldn't see why they hadn't known each other long, she was just in another relationship a couple months prior.

This Menz guy was average in looks at best. He was very light skinned with freckles, he had pretty light brown eyes and thick lips. Sutton often questioned her friends' choice in men, but she had her type, even though Sutton didn't understand it. Piper was beautiful, skin the color of brown sugar, her short hair made her face look slenderer than it really was, and her body was sick. She was short as shit but was stacked in all the right places. Her friend was a baddie.

"Baby chill we were just dancing."

"Baby?" the girl that was accompanying them said and Piper looked at her like she was crazy. "Well don't you think that it's a good idea that you tell *baby* that you gotta *baby* on the way? Oh, and how about you tell her that I'm ya girl." The tall thin girl placed her hands on her nonexistent hips and rolled her neck real hood rat style.

Piper laughed, we both knew what that meant, she was about to go off. She didn't think anything about this situation was funny, she was trying to calm herself down. Her leg shaking was telling Sutton that if something about this conversation didn't change quick there would be no calming her down.

"Menzell!" the girls heard being yelled across the barn. When they turned around to see who it was, Sutton came face to face with the scary guy she saw when they first got there. He smirked at her and her panties immediately became soaked. "What the fuck you got going on? You know we don't do the unnecessary drama. Handle that before I have to handle it for you."

Kahleno's attention went right to the light skin beauty that he saw the minute she walked through the door. It was something about her that commanded the room and his attention.

Kahleno didn't know if it was her blemish free skin, those light brown eyes or maybe it was the way her long legs filled out the white material of the skinny jeans she had on. Whatever it was it worked, and he wanted to know more about who she was, but now was not the time.

"My bad cuz," Menz said knowing that he had fucked up yet again. He was already on thin ice with his cousins, having messed up the shipment that he was supposed to handle for his trap. So, this only added to the backlash he was sure to get from them. Especially seeing as though he wasn't blood. His dad married into the Maler family and that got him the privileges that he did have but he could feel his chances were running out.

"Yeah you do that." Kahleno slowly turned to the direction of the two beauties, one that he had seen with his cousin before and the other he wished he had on his team. He winked at Sutton before taking his place back on the other side of the room surrounded by a flock of women.

Sutton took in his smooth chocolate skin and the way his thick, solid frame filled out the navy-blue Tom Ford suit. The suit matched with the cleanest pair of navy gator's she had ever seen. His Tom Ford cologne lingered as she fantasized about running her naturally gifted fingers through his thick curly hair.

"And you can stop staring at him, he's taken. My sister got him on lock," April, the skinny bitch that was with Menz said to Sutton.

"April shut the fuck up!" Menz barked, and she sighed and stood there like a little puppy.

"Yeah I'm out." Piper threw up the deuces and headed for the door. She was not for being played, especially for someone who wasn't even on her level, she knew that she was a beautiful woman inside and out.

She just hated that she spent so much time with him. Granted they had only knew each other for a little over two months but she felt connected to him. Almost like God put him in her path for a reason.

"Let me holla at you Piper." Menz reached out to Piper who drew her hand back and shook her head.

"What you mean?" April threw her hands on her hips. She had been seeing Menz for almost a year now and even though the two weren't exclusive she was his constant. Now that she had just found out that she was pregnant she figured that that would solidify a spot in his life but that was the furthest thing from the truth.

"April shut the fuck up and take yo ass on somewhere before you piss me off." Menz gave her a look that said *get on* and she did just that.

Piper watched as April made her way on the other side of the barn and sat the hell down somewhere. Piper shook her head, she knew that there was not a chance in hell that she would ever work with Menz, she wished like hell he would talk to her like that without her popping him in the mouth.

"Look, I hate that she did all that shit. I can assure you that she ain't pregnant, at least not by me anyway. I just want you to hear me out." Sutton looked at Piper who looked down and then back at Menz before she looked at her friend.

"You have got to be shitting me Piper?" Sutton gave her best friend a knowing look. "He just disrespected you in front of all of these people and you want to... you know what... do you sis." Sutton waved Piper off. She didn't even want to waste her breath; her place was not to judge her but to be there for her when shit hit the fan and she was sure it would.

Piper knew that she was settling for less with Menz and she knew that he was lying about not being with that girl, but she felt she owed it to herself to hear him out. Sutton walked over to the bar and vowed to wait for no more than thirty minutes for Piper to bring her ass before she left her there with that yella nigga.

CHAPTER TWO

Hello Beautiful

"Damn Kahleno, you gone burn a whole through that bitch the way you staring at her." Cassidy, Kahleno's older brother said from the seat beside him. Kahleno looked at Cassidy and then focused his attention on the light skinned beauty.

He had never been that intrigued by a woman before, he was so used to women flocking to him because of who he was and the fact that she didn't was baffling to him. He never thought that he would like that because he worked hard for his name, but it was turning out to be a turn on.

The Maler brothers were not only the most ruthless drug dealers on the east coast, they were the smartest. It wasn't much that they hadn't seen, done, or mastered. They ran their operation right from the family farm that was passed down to them from their father, who got it from his. They came from a long line of farmer/drug dealers.

The drug game came easy for them and they were good at it, it was in their blood. The only thing that their father and grandfather didn't have was a way to wash their money, so it made it hard for them to expand the way Cassidy, Kahleno, and Adorée had. The brothers turned the farm into one of the biggest meat districts the east coast had ever seen, servicing the majority of the restaurants in the Metro-Charlotte area.

"She's acting like she don't even know who you are," AD said from the other side of Kahleno with a smirk on his face. He had one of his stripper bitches in his lap, she seemed bored, hell she probably was. AD hadn't said shit to her the entire time we were all sitting here.

"She knows who I am, she's just trying to play hard." Kahleno said and sat back in his seat as Lexus climbed back in his lap.

He looked at her and shook his head. Lexus was April's sister and they fucked around every now and then. He met her through Menz, he should have known better because Menz's taste in women was just horrible but since all of his options was tripping, he smashed, and she been popping up ever since.

Cassidy laughed because just like April, Lexus was thirsty as hell. She wanted to be claimed by anyone with money, but she would never have a chance with Kahleno because in his eyes she wasn't worth more than a fuck and an Uber home. She didn't fit into his "lifestyle".

"Aye cousins!" Menz joined the men back in the section. The minute he walked in April was right behind him. Menzell didn't miss the dirty looks he received from his cousins, but he tried his best to pretend like everything was good.

"Who is that?" Kahleno said ignoring his cousin's attempt to rectify the situation. They were tired of him and his constant fuck ups, it was like he couldn't do shit right. HE was on his last leg with them and he didn't even know it.

"Who? That bitch Piper?" April smacked her lips and placed her hands on her hips. Before Kahleno had the chance to address, Cas was on her.

"Yo you can get the fuck out with all that bullshit. No one was even talking to you. Menz get your off-brand Barbie under control before you both piss me the fuck off." Cassidy yelled. He hated a ghetto ass chick, one with no home training. That's why he was so selective in the women he fucked with. *A woman can be a man's down fall*, that's what he always said. "Ghetto ass hood rat." Cas didn't try to mask his ill feeling towards April, he's never liked her and didn't understand why Menz kept bringing her around.

"You gone let him talk to me like that?" April asked Menz who swallowed hard and focused his attention back on Kahleno causing all of the brothers to laugh. Menz knew better.

"Nah the chick that's with her." Lexus adjusted herself in his lap and followed his stare to the sexy woman who had commanded his attention the entire time that she had been there. She had tried every attempt to get his focus on her but to no avail.

"That's Pipers home girl, she owns that Salon uhhh shit I forget the name." Kahleno shot Menz a look and he flipped through his mental rolodex trying to figure out the name of the salon before he caused more trouble for himself. "Chamber of Beauty, that's it. Yeah Piper is a makeup artist there."

Kahleno nodded his head and he searched for her in the crowd, he stretched his neck trying his best to find her and he couldn't find her anywhere. Lexus ran her hands through his hair while licking her lips. Grabbing her wrists, he scowled at her.

"Do I fucking play that?" he said through gritted teeth. She rolled her eyes and he bent her arm back causing a pain to shoot through it. "Do I fucking allow you to put your fucking hands in my hair?"

"No! Owww, you're hurting me Kahleno!" he let her go and then pushed her off of his lap causing her to hit the floor. Standing up he brushed off his suit and then looked down at the desperate woman. Lexus wasn't an ugly girl, she actually had potential if she wasn't so damn thirsty. Kahleno thought the shit was cute at first but now it was starting to be too much. Shaking his head, he walked off in the direction of where he last saw Sutton.

In the bathroom, Sutton was standing in the mirror taking in her appearance. She had to admit the white pants that she had on fit her amazingly and the red crop top that showed a little boob action was tastefully sexy. She was in a league of her own and she knew it, confidence had never been an issue, dealing with fucked up men had.

She ran her fingers through her long, sandy brown hair and then swept one side over to the other and let it rest on her shoulder. Women paid good money to have hair like hers and she took pride in the fact that she grew it all herself.

"Girl are you ready to go or what?" Sutton asked suddenly feeling the urge to go home. She just wanted to slide in her bed and cuddle up under her warm covers. She was starting to cramp already from the morning after pill that she stopped and got before they got there.

"You suck for you to be so young." Piper rolled her eyes. "You should really live a little."

"Well next time take me to a club where we ain't surrounded by fuck niggas and I might actually have a good time."

"Who the fuck you calling a fuck nigga?" Kahleno said eaves dropping on the pair from outside of the bathroom. Sutton looked on shocked, one because this crazy nigga was in the women's bathroom and two because he was addressing her like it was okay to be listening to her private conversation.

"That was a private conversation thank you." Sutton said with her hands on her hips.

"This my shit, ain't no privacy in this bitch." Suttons eyes followed the seam of his suit down to the very visible print in his pants back up to the sexy smirk on his face. She shook her head and blushed under his stare, he had her off her square.

Sutton had a whole man at home, she didn't know why she was sitting here smiling at another one that would more than likely cause her more problems than her own. Shaking her head, she turned back to the mirror and finished *freshening up*.

Kahleno loved the way Sutton's thick ass poked out in her white jeans, how she was small up top and thick on the bottom, possessing a small gap between her legs showing that she was slightly bowlegged. He imagined himself picking her up and sitting her on the marble counter top while he ate her until she begged him to stop. He chuckled at the thought.

Walking up behind her, he pressed his semi hard dick against her ass causing her to jump but not move. She stared at him through the mirror, her voice was caught in her throat so all she could do was stare. She wanted to tell him to back the fuck up because she wasn't a cheater and that she had a man, but nothing would come out.

A soft moan left her lips and she didn't mean for it to. Piper sat back and watched the exchange of the two and she slowly made her way out of the bathroom to give them a minute alone. She didn't feel like Trouble was good enough for her friend and any chance to get her out of his grasps she took it and she knew that Kahleno was that nigga and could give Sutton the world if she wanted it. She knew she had no room to judge but that was her friend and she loved her, so her stopping this wasn't even an option.

"You're invading my personal space." She said finally finding her voice, it wasn't loud, but it was audible.

"Would you like me to move?" Kahleno leaned down and

said against her ear causing her pussy to leak more than it already was. She was sure that the thong she had on was no good after this. "All you have to do is tell me to move."

Sutton didn't know what she wanted him to do, she was stuck in a trance that belonged to a man whose name she didn't even know. Kahleno's hand moved to her waist line, down her thighs and then back around to her ass where he leaned back enough to get a squeeze but not enough to create any distance for her to get away.

Clearing her throat, she attempted to stand her ground, "I think you should..." She started.

"Should what?" shit happened so fast that Sutton didn't even know what was going on, he had turned her around and stuck his tongue down her throat. The kiss started off slow and sensual and before either of them knew it had got deep and nasty.

Kahleno, like Sutton was doing things that he normally wouldn't do. Now fucking a bitch in the bathroom was normal for him, this was the first place he had fucked Lexus, but he wasn't with the kissing thing. He didn't trust women enough to put his lips on them, but he found himself trying to examine her tonsils. They both were breathing hard and was oblivious to the fact that they had company.

"There you go baby, what..." Lexus said out loud purposely trying to get their attention. She had saw him come in here a while ago, but when he failed to come out, she knew that she needed to go in to see what the fuck he was doing.

She was not about to sit back and let some bitch cash in

on the check that she had been trying to cash. She had done everything that she could possibly do to get noticed by Kahleno, she's never had to work that hard to get a man. Lexus was finally starting to feel like her hard work was starting to get her noticed by Kahleno but here this new bitch comes.

Sutton snapped out of her lustrous state and pulled back from the kiss, but her eyes never left Kahleno's and his never left hers. The connection was so strong that even though Sutton wanted to ignore it and get away from him, she couldn't. She was stuck, it was like she saw her whole future in his eyes in that moment.

"I think I should go."

"Fuck that," he grabbed her hand and put it on his hard dick and held it there when she tried to pull it away. He didn't give a fuck that Lexus was standing there watching the entire thing, he had no respect for her, and he felt like she should know that by now. "You see what you did? You think you about to leave me like this?"

"I'm sure there is some thirsty hoe ready and willing to handle that for you." Sutton sassed aggravated that they had been interrupted and pissed off because her conscious found its way into her mind and heart making her feel bad. Kahleno smirked and leaned in and kissed her again, making his dick jump.

"Does that feel like it wants anybody but you?"

Sutton inadvertently squeezed Kahleno's dick that was still in her hand. As bad as she wanted to fuck the shit out of him, she couldn't. She had never cheated on Trouble before tonight and she couldn't even explain why she let Kahleno get that close to her. She shook her head and tried to get down, but he wouldn't let her.

"Get the fuck out Lexus!"

"No, you don't have to go anywhere." Sutton held her hand up. Kahleno looked at Lexus with a *do what the fuck I said* look and she headed to the door. "No, listen I let you get me off my square but I'm not that kind of girl. I'm not about to fuck you in a bathroom of a barn turned club, that ain't even me. I don't know what you did to me or what y'all putting in them drinks but you definitely got me bugging." Her eyes met Kahleno's again. "And the fucked-up part is I don't even know your name." she shook her head at herself, Trouble really had her head fucked up.

"The man that's going to change your life for the better, but for now you can call me Kahleno." He smiled at her and she could have melted right then and there. "Do you not know who I am?" The question took Sutton by surprise.

"Should I?" Sutton cocked her head to the side. She was trying to see if she had seen him somewhere before, but she hadn't. Kahleno was somewhat offended but intrigued at the same time. A lazy grin slowly spread across his face.

"I like that!" he nodded his head.

"Like what?"

"The fact that you don't give a fuck who I am and you're not willing to go against your morals just to be with a man like me." Sutton searched his eyes for an answer to the riddle that he was saying. "You'll find out soon enough," he said reading her mind.

Sutton sighed, "No, no I won't!" she put her hands in her sandy colored hair and then ran them down her face. "I have a fiancé." It was like the words wouldn't leave her lips. She knew that she was wrong, and she hated to admit it. "I shouldn't even be here." Lexus began to laugh drawing a death stare from Kahleno.

Kahleno removed her hands from her face, grabbed the back of her head, and pulled her to him, his tongue invaded her mouth once again and she allowed him to. It felt too good to stop him, all she kept thinking about is how his thick tongue would feel against her clit.

"I don't give a fuck about you having no got damn man, as long as you're not married the way I see it, you're fair game. When I want that pussy to be mine, that pussy will be mine and I have no doubts about that." He said against her lips making her clit throb. After assaulting her lips one more time he grabbed her hands and helped her off of the counter, but still not giving her enough space to escape him. "Lexus what the fuck you still standing there for? I ain't ya nigga."

"But I thought we were chilling?"

"No yo desperate ass came up here with your sister, in hopes of going home with me. I didn't invite you here. If and when I want my dick sucked, I'll let you know. Until then get the fuck out of my face."

Lexus' face dropped, she had hopes of getting to spend the night with Kahleno at his condo like the last time. He was so drunk he forgot to get up and call her an Uber, she even woke up with his arms around her. In her mind if she could get a few more of those nights then maybe she could lock him down or catch him slipping enough to get pregnant, like April had.

"Um yeah I gotta go." Sutton wiggled her way from between Kahleno and the counter. Before she could get too far, he snatched her up and enclosed her in his arms.

"Don't ever get it twisted, I want you, I just fuck her, there's a difference." There was so much conviction in his voice that it almost scared Sutton. "I'll see you later." He said matter-of-factly.

Sutton walked by the Lexus chick who was giving her the death stare, she shook her head at her desperate ass and went in search of Piper. They needed to go and quick before she ended up doing something that she would more than likely regret. Or would she?

~

On the other side of the barn, Piper was letting Menz disrespect her in the worse way. Not only was he fucking her behind a barn, but he was doing it raw and while a girl that claimed to be his baby mama was in the building looking for him.

She had been in so many bad relationships that it was hard for her to see that she was being played and degraded. The fact that she fell in love so hard and fast made it damn near impossible for her to see any of the signs because by the time they show up she's already all the way in and be dumb for yet another no-good man

"Yes Menz, fuck baby right there." He didn't have the biggest dick in the world, he was average, and he barely knew what to do with it but Piper made it work.

"Damn why yo pussy so tight." He said through clenched teeth. Menz had to admit that Piper was the only woman that he had ever been with that pussy smelled and felt like it should. He was used to fucking with them project chicks that really didn't give a damn but neither did he.

"Go faster baby, that's my spot." Piper hated that she had to tell Menz what to do to please her during sex, she always got her orgasm, but she had to tell him how to give it to her. She felt like he should know her body and pay attention enough to know exactly what to do to get her there. "No baby over a little, yeah yeah just like that. Fuck I'm about to cum."

"Hell yeah baby, don't nobody fuck you like I do!" Menz taunted. "Can't nobody get in that spot like I do, can they? Can they?"

"You lost it baby, back over to the right." She ignored his boasting and tried to get him to get to where she needed him to be to get her off. "Yes, yes god yessssss!" she closed her eyes tight as she felt her orgasm hit the pit of her gut and the pour out on to his dick like a fountain.

"Got damn, you soaked a nigga, and this shit smell good," he said still pumping in and out of her mercilessly. "Pull this nut out of yo nigga." Piper began to move her body in sync with is until he stepped back pulling out of her and jerking himself the rest of the way. At least he didn't nut in her.

Menz knew that he didn't want kids right now, which was why he was so pissed about the baby April claimed she was pregnant with. He was too busy trying to make a name for himself in the game, he loved women and wasn't trying to slow down for anyone. He looked at Piper with a lazy grin on her face. She was so beautiful to him, he just hoped that she would stick around long enough for him to sew all the royal oats that he wanted.

"Damn baby." She went to reach for her pants but was drenched with a drink in the process. Her short hair was just laid earlier today by Sutton and this bitch had just fucked it up. That was grounds for an ass whipping. Piper drew back and punched April in the face and she went tumbling to the ground.

April wasn't much of a fighter, but she could throw a drink or two. "How you out here fucking this bitch and you just ate my pussy in this same spot just hours ago? And he fucked me raw and didn't wash up." April smirked. "And I see he did the same thing to you."

"You nasty son of a bitch." Piper finished working her pants up before she turned to attack Menz. He tried to fight her off at first, but her little short ass was strong. Her little fist was connecting with his face, the more she swung the madder he got.

"Stop got damn it." he picked her up and threw her as far as his skinny ass could and that wasn't far. Piper landed on her feet and her and Menz was going toe to toe, he was fighting her like she was a man.

"What the fuck!" Sutton said as she was heading to the car to check and see if Piper was out there. She so happened to look over and saw her fighting Menz, granted she was fucking him up, but she still didn't believe that a man should be putting his hands on a woman.

The barn walls were thin, and the DJ had turned the volume down on the music because he was about to pack up for the night. Lexus had pissed Kahleno off by interrupting him so he was shutting the music down so he could go home before he chopped her up and had Cassidy feed her to the fucking hogs.

The commotion could be heard from inside and Kahleno, Cassidy, and AD ran outside to see what was going on. They took pride in not drawing a lot of attention to the farm, they had too much to lose here. There life was here, and they weren't about to lose everything over some bullshit ass drama.

Their parties were normally really lowkey, a few of their workers and their friends and that's it. As of lately Menz had been inviting too many people causing Kahleno and Cassidy to agree to shut the parties down for a while. Last thing they needed was police snooping around. They had connections and a few cops in their pockets, but they would still rather steer clear.

"Yo bitch get the fuck off of me." Menz yelled at Sutton, who was on his back beating him in the face while Piper was hitting him in his nuts and in his chest. Once Menz hit the ground Sutton and Piper started to stomp his ass out with their heels. Menz rolled around on the ground trying to get away from their attack.

"You ever hit my muthafuckin' friend again I'll kill you!" Sutton yelled out of anger.

"Fuck this bitch ass nigga!" Piper yelled taking her stiletto and driving it down in his groin. He would never touch her with his dirty dick again, so she didn't feel the need to spare it.

"Ohhhhhh you bitch! April!" he screamed like a bitch. They continued to beat his ass until the both of them were picked up and carried away from the fight. Menz rolled around on the ground, calling out for April who was nowhere to be found. That one pop to the mouth was enough for her and she knew that she needed her sister's help to handle the crazed bitch.

Piper fought hard against Cassidy's hold, but he was too strong for her. She was embarrassed and really didn't want to be around anyone right now. Especially some thick strong nigga that smelled good enough to eat.

Sutton on the other hand knew exactly whose arms she was in, she remembered those arms and the smell of his cologne. Her pussy jumped just thinking about what could have been.

"Put me down!" Piper yelled as she wiggled some more to get loose.

"Yo you better chill before yo short ass be on the floor."

Damn even this nigga voice is sexy! Piper thought to herself.

When Cas felt like she was far enough away from Menz he put her down. Piper swung around and got a good look at the sexy brother that had her all hemmed up.

His sexy low-cut fade enhanced his smooth chocolate skin, and his goatee and mustache added to his sex appeal. He was at least 6'6", towering completely over Piper and she thought that was sexy. The scowl on his face was meant to scare Piper but she welcomed it.

"Look don't be mad at me because you let that nigga disrespect you on so many levels. He invited you here while he had another bitch here because he knew that neither of you would do anything about it. He knew that he could get away with that shit because neither of you know your got damn worth. Then you let him take you around there and fuck you like a common whore with a dirty dick!" Cas shook his head.

It wasn't that he cared it's just that he thought he saw something in the brown skinned beauty that was more than what she was showing, he was somewhat disappointed. Even though he didn't know her, somewhere in the back of his mind he hoped that she was a better woman than the one she was portraying.

"Don't judge me, you don't know shit about me."

"I don't have to know you to see that you don't love yourself shorty, not acting like this. Take a step back and stop settling," Cas said and walked off shaking his head. He couldn't understand how women allowed themselves to be handled the way Menz was handling her and be okay with it. It sickened him.

Piper felt so low, if she never felt like a fool before, she did right now. She wanted to cry so bad, but she wouldn't give any of them the satisfaction. She hated herself for putting herself out there like that once again.

Sensing her girls' pain, Sutton moved in her direction grabbing her up in a hug and pulling her towards the car but not before looking back at Kahleno and leaving him with a soft smile that he would probably be thinking about for the rest of the night.

CHAPTER THREE

Disconnected

Kahleno turned the key to the home that he used to share with the mother of his 4-year-old son, Kahlil. The smell of Bath and Body Work's Hot Cocoa and Cream scented candles filled the house. That's one thing that Kahleno loved about Karson, she kept a clean house and she took good care of their son.

"Umph, I'm surprised you're here." Karson said coming from the kitchen dressed down in a pair of leggings and a sports bra. He had to admit that he had good taste in women.

"Ain't no one wanna hear that shit, where's Kahlil?"

"He was up late last night watching You Tube so he's still sleep." Karson rolled her eyes, she hated the way that Kahleno treated her. Yes, she made a mistake a while ago, but it wasn't grounds for him to keep treating her like this. Like she didn't once mean something to him.

"Well shit, just call me when he get up then. I'll take him for a haircut and my pops wanna see him, he's in town." He looked down at his phone and sent a message back to AD telling him that he would get back to him.

"I cooked, you wanna eat while you wait for him to wake up? I'm sure the second he hears your voice he'll be up!" Karson said with an ounce of hope in her voice.

Kahleno looked at Karson skeptically, she had been trying to get back with him ever since he stopped fucking with her for trying to steal his sperm. Karson had asked him for another baby because she wanted her kids to have the same father but Kahleno didn't want any more kids right now.

He wanted to be settled and preferably married before he decided to bring more kids into the world. Right now, he was focused on setting himself up so that him and his family wouldn't want for anything. He wanted his great grand kids to never have to work a day in their lives if they didn't want to and he wasn't gone stop until that happened. So, he wasn't having any more kids until then either.

Karson wasn't about to take no for an answer so when they would have sex, she would take the condom off and bring him a wet rag so he wouldn't have to get up. Kahleno thought that she was just catering to her man but one night he had to pee, so he got up right after her and watched as she took a turkey baster looking thing and took his nut out of the condom and into a medicine jar looking thing.

Karson was a nurse at a fertility clinic, so she knew the proper way to handle semen. So, she had no doubt that she could get his sperm and impregnate herself, without his permission.

The day Kahleno burst in the door and caught her was the worse day of her life. He made her feel desperate and low, to say she was embarrassed was an understatement and he's been making her pay for it ever since.

Kahleno felt like he couldn't trust her, and he wasn't going to be with anyone that he couldn't trust. With the line of work that he's in, he couldn't afford to let pussy be his downfall and he refused to.

"So long as you ain't on no bullshit." Kahleno shrugged his shoulder and headed to the table to wait for Karson to fix his plate.

She was elated to say the least, it had been so long since Kahleno had agreed to sit down with her and just be civil. Everything between them is solely about their son, if it didn't concern Kahlil, Kahleno didn't want to hear it and she had herself to thank for that.

"How is Mega doing?" Karson asked about Kahleno's father, trying to make small talk. Kahleno dropped his fork and sighed, sitting back in the chair he folded his arms across his chest and glared at her. "Damn Kah I can't even ask you a got damn question? We were together over damn near five years and I can't ask about your dad now?" she squinted her eyes throwing her fork down too.

"I knew it was some shit up with this, call me when Kahlil

get up." She hadn't even really done anything to him, just the fact that she was such a big part of his life and she betrayed him fucked with him til this day. He would never admit it though. He slid back in his chair and stood up just as his son came tearing down the stairs.

"Daddy! Daddy!" he yelled jumping into his father's arms.

Kahleno picked Kahlil up and threw him in the air and then collected him in his arms and squeezed him tight. "What's up my man?" He rubbed his fist through his son's crazy wild hair. Kahlil was the best thing to ever happen to Kahleno and he loved him more than he loved his own life. Nothing came before him, not even business and it never would.

"I wanna go with you daddy!" Kahlil said wiggling down so he could go and greet his mommy. He ran in the kitchen where she had ran off to.

She was in her feelings, all she wanted was for them to be a family. Another baby was something that she always wanted, she felt that that would make them complete, somewhat whole. Kahleno was the man that she wanted to marry eventually, and she knew it. She just thought that having another baby would solidify her chances of having forever with him.

Kahleno could hear his son asking his mom why she was crying, "Nothing baby, mommy did something bad and she feels really upset that she did it. I'll be okay though I promise."

Karson kissed her son. She hated telling him that nothing was wrong with her because she wanted him to know that it was okay to express your feelings no matter how bad it was. She just didn't know how to tell her son that she got caught trying to trap his daddy and that's why they weren't a family anymore.

Wiping her eyes, she looked down at her son, there was an innocence about him, and she prayed that he never lost it. Kahlil too, was the greatest thing in her life. She just hates that she let her selfish intentions ruin the family that he deserved.

"Well you should forgive yourself, everybody fucks up every now and then."

"Kahlil watch your mouth!" Karson and Kahleno said at the same time.

When she returned to the dining area, her face was void of any tears or emotion, but you could tell she was crying by her puffy eyes. She refused to look at me just like the many other times that we had had this same conversation.

Karson thought that Kahleno shouldn't keep holding this over her head and that he should just forget about what she did and move on with her. That was just something that he couldn't do , she was a good girl, but she had some grimy instincts that he couldn't get with. A woman that will intentionally trap a man, will intentionally set his ass up too and no one could tell him different.

"You can finish your food in peace, I'll go get him ready. Do you need me to pack anything?" her tone was defeated but it didn't move him one way or another.

"No, you know I got him set at my crib." Nodding her

head, she headed up the stairs, Kahleno's eyes were glued to her ass the entire time.

Karson was a natural beauty, she had the lightest skin to be fully black. The freckles that lined her nose were so sexy to Kahleno, he remembered running his finger along them when she was mad at him. She was built like the beauty he met the other night. They were kind of similar if he would have to say so himself. He had a type and Karson was definitely that.

Kahleno thought that Karson was it for him, he still did his thing and fucked other women from time to time, but he never put that shit in her face, and he made sure she never knew about it. Til this day, if you asked her if Kahleno was loyal to her, her answer would always be yes, he had that much respect for her. Kahleno knew that she could be his forever until she fucked up his trust.

Thirty minutes later, Kahlil was fully dressed and ready to go. "Hey man where's your phone?" Karson said. She normally liked him to leave it at home, because that gave her a reason to talk to Kahleno but right now she was in her feelings.

Kahleno chuckled knowing what was up, he shook his head and headed for the door with his son in tow. That was the main reason he avoided sitting down with her or conversing with her on something other than their son.

"Tell Mega I said hello, and your mom too." she smiled and shut the door behind Kahleno after waving goodbye to her son. "Why won't he just forgive me?"

Karson threw herself against the door and slid down it. She threw her head in her hands and cried until her eyes were sore. When she did what she did she thought that she was doing what was best for them. When she got pregnant with Kahlil, Kahleno didn't want any kids but he was there every step of the way. The minute he saw his son, she had never saw his eyes light up like they did. It warmed her heart so much.

She wanted to recreate that moment with a new baby and further solidify her spot in his life, but her plan back fired. Now she wished she would have just left well enough alone, she would still have the life that she dreamed of. Now she felt like an outsider in her own damn family, she felt so disconnected from him and alone.

CHAPTER FOUR

Intrigued

Piper drug herself out of bed, she knew that it was almost the weekend and she would have an abundance of clients coming in to get their face beat to snag the biggest boss they could find. For the last week she had been held up in her house nursing the black eye Menz gave her the night they went to the party.

She hated herself for how she let him treat her and now she was sitting here not only nursing a black eye but taking a prescription for Chlamydia. Go figure. She should have been more careful with who she spread herself with and unprotected.

Had her mom been any kind of mother and taught her about what she should and shouldn't accept from men, then maybe she would have had a chance. Natalie was a woman that accepted any and everything from a man, as long as they were paying her bills, she was with whatever and though Piper has made away for herself she still has that same mindset. The only difference was, Piper was looking for love instead of a come up.

Walking through the doors of *Chamber of Beauty* all eyes were on Piper. The nosey stylist stayed in somebody business so when she walked through, she flipped them all off. The women all wondered where Piper had been, they had all heard different stories about what happened to her, but they wanted to hear it for themselves.

Piper knew what they were all thinking, which is why her glasses stayed on her face and she made her way back to her office. She had clients coming in soon, she didn't have time to cater to nosey bitches.

"How you feeling P?" Sutton asked as she shut my door to block out channel 9 news, or her staff if you wanted to be technical. She came by every day to make sure that Piper was good. That was her girl and she wouldn't let her go through this alone, Sutton just prayed that this was a lesson learned for her.

Piper thanked God that Sutton was her boss, that's the only way that she was able to stay down as long as she did and not have any consequences for it.

"I'm good, I still got a dark mark under my fucking eye, I was able to cover it with makeup though." Piper shrugged her shoulders.

She was trying her best to downplay the situation, it was

getting harder and harder. Deep down Piper was hurt because she kept allowing herself to be treated as less than what she deserved. There was no judgement on Sutton's part and that's what made Piper respect her as a friend.

Sutton knew that her best friend was feeling a way and even if she doesn't want to talk about it, she was still gonna be there for her. Sutton leaned over and hugged Piper with all her might and walked back out to tend to the client that she had in her chair. She knew that when her friend was ready to talk, she would be right there with her.

"Welcome to Chamber of Beauty!" Sutton said without looking up to see who was entering. When the person didn't respond she looked up and into the eyes of the gentleman that almost made her forget that she was due to be married to another man.

Suttons eyes danced around Kahleno's attire, just like the last time she saw him he had on a tailored Tom Ford suit except this one was light blue in color and it brought out his dark colored skin. His goatee was neatly trimmed, and his sideburns connected perfectly. The man was sexy as fuck and she couldn't deny that.

"Damn how can *I* help... you?" Sunny asked from the station to the left of Sutton drawing a nasty look from her. Sunny's eyes undressed every inch of Kahleno and she was making her way back up until Sutton cleared her throat.

"How about we be professional!" Sutton didn't know why she felt so territorial over a man that she had just met a few days ago but yet here she was about to hand out pink slips because Sunny was getting out of pocket. "How can I help you today?"

"You don't want me to answer that question, not right now and definitely not right here." Kahleno watched as Sutton suddenly became uncomfortable, the sweat that formed above her perfectly sculpted brows made Kahleno's man grow.

It was crazy to him that just the little things about her were starting to become things that he desired. The way her doe shaped eyes became low when she was trying not to give in to his advance like right now, or the way her cheeks got a pink tint to them when she was heating up, just to name a few. He gave her a lopsided grin and she blushed, gaining a lot of chatter from the clients in the shop.

"Kahleno!" she warned.

"I love how you say my name, say it again." Kahleno teased and again she blushed.

"I thought I heard a familiar voice," Piper came out of the back of the shop and reached her hand out to shake Kahleno's. She hadn't been around him often but when she had he always seemed cool, he had a smart-ass mouth but was cool none the less.

Kahleno took a good look at Piper's face and got pissed all over again. After she left that night, Kahleno showed Menzell how it felt to be hit by someone not of equal strength, in other words he got his ass beat. It still didn't take away the anger that he felt, he was always taught never to hit a woman and he expected everyone that was in his circle to abide by that too.

"Yo you need to stay away from that nigga, real talk. He a bum ass nigga, he might talk a good game but the nigga ain't shit. Them my peoples and I'm telling you straight up. Don't no real man sit up and go toe to toe with no woman and almost get his ass beat," Kahleno said trying not to laugh but the minute Sutton snickered it was a losing battle.

"Ion be playing with these niggas." For the first time in days, Piper laughed, and it felt good. Kahleno was right, fuck Menz he didn't deserve her.

"Hell, no you was whopping his ass for a minute there, that's why we didn't jump in right away but check it, still, never put yo self in a situation like that again. If he was a real nigga, he would have hurt you," he said, and Piper nodded in agreeance then disappeared back in the back where she was.

Sutton stood back and admired what he was saying. She honestly didn't think that she would see him after that night, and she had just got to the point that she didn't think about him and how he made her feel. Him standing right in front of her right now had her conflicted, especially now seeing that her and Trouble were at each other's throats.

He failed to come home two days in a row and his excuse was that he had to make some of the money back that he lost because Sutton wouldn't give him any. The crazy thing about that is he came home with no money and further in debt.

"That was nice."

"I'ma nice nigga."

"Shit you can be my nigga, I'm just saying," Sunny butted in.

Kahleno looked at her and immediately knew that she was the kind of woman that he vowed to always stay away from. She was built just right, small waist, wide hips, flat stomach, but her mouth was ratchet and she looked to be a messy bitch.

Everything that Kahleno thought about Sunny was right, she was young and dumb. She stayed in everyone's business, if you wanted to know anything on the street then she was the one that you would go to. She couldn't count the number of times she had to fight because she was too deep in someone's business.

Choosing to ignore her, Kahleno walked over to where Sutton was standing and sat down in her chair that was currently empty. All eyes were on him, but it didn't move him one way or another because his attention was on Sutton.

He winked to fuck with them and every woman in attendance damn near melted and wondered what it would be like to be with one of the Maler brothers. Unbeknownst to Sutton, she was dealing with a hood legend.

"What are you doing? I have appointments." Sutton swung the chair around so that they were facing each other. Bad move on her part because Kahleno leaned up and grabbed her legs and lightly squeezed, drawing everyone's attention to them. "You have to stop, I told you I was engaged."

"What does you being engaged have to do with this feeling that the both of us are feeling right now? If you can explain that to me then I will get up and walk up out of here and out of your life forever." Sutton's bottom lip made its way into her mouth and she nibbled on it. Kahleno knew that she was drawn to him like he was to her, it was unexplainable, but it was definitely there.

"Kahleno I...I" Sutton started but was interrupted by the cutest little laugh.

"Daddy! Daddy! Daddy!" Kahlil came running into the shop with an older version of Kahleno. Sutton looked back and forth between the duo and couldn't believe how much all three of them looked alike. "Damn daddy who is this? She's sexy."

"Watch your damn mouth Kahlil!" Mega, Kahleno's father told his grandson, silently agreeing with him. Kahleno laughed because his son was so outspoken, much like he was when he was that age and now. "Sorry PopPop, she's very pretty, daddy is she your woman? If not, can she be my woman?"

"Not yet son but I'm trying to make that happen." Kahleno smiled big causing Sutton's cheeks to take on a red hue. She shook her head and turned away so she could get herself together.

She was indeed smitten, even though she knew it wasn't right. She loved Trouble but she was starting to be over his shit. It was stressing her out, his gambling wasn't healthy for either of them.

"You know my saying son, if you want it, take it." Mega shrugged his shoulders and looked around the salon at all the thirsty women. He knew that none of the other women in this establishment could exist in the world of a Maler, but the young lady standing in front of him, he approved of.

"Well shit, if she don't want to be your woman then I will," *Sunny started up again.*

"My daddy don't like rapid hoes," Kahlil said trying to say ratchet hoes but mispronounced it. Sutton could hold on to her laughter anymore, Kahlil was hilarious to her and she was loving his little company.

"Kahlil Maler wa—"

"I know, I know, watch my mouth." He hunched his shoulders and dropped his head. He was pouting and Sutton thought that was the sweetest thing that she had ever seen.

"Hey, how are you cutie? I'm Sutton." She reached her hand out and he accepted with a smile. "You're Kahlil, right?" he nodded his head. "Well thank you for the compliment and I think you are the cutest thing that I have ever seen."

"Besides his daddy," Kahleno said still sitting in her chair.

"Even cuter than your daddy." Kahlil blushed and crossed his little arms across his chest to match his dad and his grandfather.

"He's bad as hell is what he is," Sunny thought she said under her breath, but they heard her. Kahlil opened his mouth to say something, but Sutton cut him off.

"Umm so what brings you in?" she looked between the three different versions of Maler, finally resting on Kahleno.

"I wanted you to braid my hair," Kahleno said. "I heard you were the best. So, I want you to do it but not now," he smirked, and Sutton sighed. She knew where he was going with this and as good as it may feel at the moment, she knew it was wrong and her loyalty was with Trouble.

"Kahleno, I don't think that's a good idea."

He reached into his jacket pocket and slammed down a stack of money on her work station. Sutton's eyes stretched wide and her mouth opened and shut. She shook her head while squeezing her eyes shut and then opening them again.

Envy quickly rose inside of Sunny. She knew that she could do so much with that money. She could lace her kids and buy her a few good wigs. She couldn't wait to put Trouble up on game.

Sutton stared at the money, she knew that it would definitely put her in a position to be back on top. She could pay up her mortgage before her father found out about it, which was the last thing that she wanted. Plus, she had the hair show that she wanted to do and thanks to Trouble she didn't have the money.

"You're making this really hard Kahleno," Sutton whined.

"I know, that's the point," he laughed along with his dad.

"Fine, come back tomorrow at two."

"No, I can't do it until after eight," he smirked. "I have a business to run." He winked.

Sutton thought about the money again and not taking that money was not an option. It was either take the money or dip into her business fund, which she vowed that she would never do and so far, she's stuck to that. She needed that money, she was just going to have to practice some self-control.

"Who owns this shop?" Mega asked looking around.

"I do," Sutton beamed. Chamber of Beauty was her baby, she poured all of her sweat and tears into this place. That and the fact it was built with her mother's insurance money made it that much more special. She would rather have her mom than the shop but since that was impossible this was the next best thing. She felt like her mom was a part of making all of this happen, and she cherished it.

"Amazing job, daughter in law." Sutton got choked on her own spit and went into a fit of coughing. Mega smiled along with Kahleno.

Mega knew that whenever his sons want something it's not much that could stop them from getting it. He could see that Kahleno wanted this young woman and from what he could see he supported that decision. He was a good judge of character and Sutton brought nothing but good vibes.

"Can you do my hair too?" Kahlil looked up at Sutton.

"I gotta little time, what would you like me to do?" she asked him bending down so that she was eye level with him.

"You can stand up, I like my women tall." The shop erupted in laughter. Kahlil was something else and he stayed getting in trouble for his mouth. Sutton thought it was cute minus the cursing.

"Well okay, daddy can you move?" Sutton said looking in Kahleno's direction. His tongue swept across his bottom lip before he slid out of the seat making sure he touched her on his way out.

"Falling in line already," he whispered in her ear as he made his way to his son so he could lift him into the chair.

Sutton tried to ignore him, but the seat of her panties couldn't be ignored, she was intrigued by this man and there was no way around it. Sutton got specific instructions about how to cut his hair from Kahlil. He wanted a mohawk with designs on the side, but not too many.

The clippers and scissors were her best friends, she knew her way around a nice cut. She twisted and turned him in the chair, listening to his stories about the school that he went to. Her side was starting to hurt she laughed so much, Kahlil was a character and he was very intelligent to only be four years old.

Kahleno couldn't help but admire the way that Sutton and Kahlil had taken to each other. It was like they had known each other for years and he was really enjoying it. So much so that he didn't want it to end and couldn't wait until tomorrow when he got to see her again.

"Alright, all done. What ya think?" she turned him towards the mirror. "How did I do?"

"Ahhhh that's fresh!" he brushed his hand down the sides of his hair taking in the designs that she etched in. "Daddy can we come here all the time?"

"Oh yeah, we'll be here often," Kahleno said laughing. Reaching into his pocket he peeled off five one hundred-dollar bills and handed them to her. "Keep the change." She opened her mouth to tell him that was too much money and that she actually wanted to do it for free because she had such a good time, but he held his hands up. "That's for you to get something nice to wear tomorrow and I'll bring dinner."

"Whoa, slow ya roll. This is not a date." Sutton held her hands up.

"Okay." He smirked and slipped his hands in his pocket and nodded for Kahlil to follow him.

"It was nice meeting you Sutton, I'll see you tomorrow!" he smiled.

"No, the hell you won't Kahlil, little cock blocking ass."

"You the cock blocker daddy, she don't even like you. You saw we was vibing. You hating bruh!" Kahlil caused the shop to go into an uproar again. Sutton chuckled and waved bye. Everyone was still laughing but then it was like the room stopped.

Sutton spun around to see what had happened and that's when she witnessed the exchange between Kahleno and Trouble. Moving her eyes back and forth between the two she could feel her arm pits get moist. How in the hell did they know each other?

"What's up Trouble, how them numbers running?" Kahleno was burning up on the inside. Trouble owed Kahleno money, only owed him a measly twenty grand but that wasn't the point. It was the principle and if he let him slide then it was only a matter of time before niggas was coming with the bullshit.

"It's all good man, I'll be by to see you later." Trouble knew that shit was about to hit the fan if he didn't find a way to pay them the twenty g's that he owed.

Kahleno looked from Trouble to Sutton and the nervous look on her face pissed him off. He was putting two and two together and his fist balled inadvertently. "Tell me that ain't yo fiancé."

Sutton didn't say anything because she was beyond embarrassed and not just because she was just flirting with another man in her shop and now her fiancé was there but because Kahleno was the one that Trouble owed money to. Kahleno looked at her with sympathetic eyes because she didn't know who it was she was dealing with. He was a snake and he didn't give a fuck about her. He had been holed up with one of their workers the earlier part of the week.

"Don't make me come looking for you Trouble, you don't want that my man."

Without another word he left, leaving Sutton there lost in her thoughts, she couldn't even stand to look at Trouble right now. She headed to her office in the back with Trouble hot on her heels. He needed to know how she *knew* Kahleno and why was he there.

"Sut, you good?" Piper yelled after her when she saw her run by her make up area. She started to leave her client and go after her until she saw Trouble not too far behind. Sucking her teeth, she turned her back as he passed.

She knew that Trouble was no good for her, he didn't mean her no good and if Sutton didn't wake up and see that shit for herself, Piper was scared that he was gonna take her down with him.

"How do you know him?" Trouble said the minute he was back in the office with Sutton and the door was closed. The last thing he needed was for people to hear that he had been fucking up. Sunny being the main one, Sutton didn't know that he was smashing her every chance he got and to her he was the man. That's where some of that money that he took from their account went.

"NO! The fucking question is how do *you* know him and don't feed me no bullshit either Trouble, because you been on a lot of that." Sutton's hands found her hips and she spun around and faced him.

"That's what you wore to work, what you was expecting that nigga or something?" The high waisted skinny jeans accentuated her ass, had it sitting up real nice and the cut off white top that read *Chamber of Beauty* showcased her small waist and plump breasts.

Laughter left her lips, not because anything was funny but because she was trying to calm herself down before things went all the way south. When her eyes met his again, he was still looking at her waiting for an answer on the bullshit ass question he asked.

"He came to get his hair braided, I don't know him," she said giving half-truths, the fact that they had another encounter before this didn't feel like it was relevant at the time. "I didn't have time to braid it, so he made an appointment, I cut his son's hair. That's it. Now what the fuck was he talking about?" She pointed towards the door like he was still sitting there.

"Nothing!"

"Still fucking lying!" Sutton threw her hands up. "You ain't gone be satisfied until *nothing* is not enough anymore."

"Look I got some business with him that's it." She dropped her head.

"So, what you saying is you owe him some money?" she asked, and he said nothing. Already knowing the answer to the question, she didn't even wait for him to answer. "How much?"

"That shit don't even matter, just know you ain't braiding that nigga hair. Fuck that, he got money. He can find anybody to braid his bitch ass hair. What the fuck you gotta do it for?"

"I don't tell you how to do you, so you don't tell me how to do me. He paid me five hundred dollars to cut his sons hair, so yeah, I am gonna braid his hair because I need the money. You ain't doing shit but taking money out of our household so you have no say in how the fuck I put it back!" Sutton pointed her perfectly manicured finger in his face. "Unless you got the money for the bank?"

"Give me that money and I'll have it by the end of the night." Again, Sutton laughed.

"YOU DUMB AS FUCK IF YOU THINK I'M GIVING YOU ANYTHING TO BLOW! HOW ABOUT YOU GET A FUCKING JOB AND BE A GOT DAMN MAN!" She yelled loud enough for the entire shop to hear. Mad was an understatement so she really didn't give a fuck who heard what or who said what.

"Damn that nigga got you bugging like that?" he took a step back. "Let me find out."

"No, you let me find out where the fuck you was when you disappeared! Huh? What's up with that Trouble? I'm so sick and tired of you. I'm trying to hold up my end of the relationship, but I swear you making it hard as fuck." There was a look in Sutton's eyes that Trouble hadn't seen before, and he didn't know what it was, but he didn't like it.

Sighing hard, Trouble knew that he had no leg to stand on. He knew that he had been on some bullshit lately, he just figured that Sutton would have his back. He knew that she had the money to pay the bank and to fix his debt in her business account, she just refused to touch it. Hell, she could even ask her father, she was just being stubborn.

"I'ma let you cool off. Can you put some money in the account so that I can grab something to eat?" Lowering her head, she shook it for the twentieth time today. Sutton covered her head with her hands and let out a muffled scream. "Aight, I'll see you at home."

Trouble was about to turn away, but something caught his attention. It was a wad of money in the side pocket of Sutton's bag. When they first got in the room, he noticed that she grabbed her bag and put something in it, but he didn't pay attention to what.

While her head was still down, he snatched the wad and made his way out the door and the shop. He would never hear the end of this but when he came home a rich man all would be forgiven.

"Hey girl you good?" Piper said easing her way inside the office the minute she saw Trouble leave.

"Girrrrllllll! You will never believe the shit that just happened."

Piper pulled up a chair and listened while Sutton laid out the events of the last hour, she didn't even realize that her appointment was out there waiting on her. Lucky for her Icelynn was chill and wouldn't dare let anyone but Sutton touch her hair.

"Did he leave the money?" Piper looked around and Sutton laughed.

"No silly, he just paid me..." Her words trailed off as she realized the pocket that she had put the five hundred dollars in was turned inside out. "I know this nigga didn't steal from me." Tears welled up in her eyes and slowly spilled onto her face. "Kahleno paid me five hundred dollars to cut his son's hair but he put the wad back in his pocket and set his appointment that he's bringing dinner to. The money was in my pocket until I got back here, and I put it in my pocketbook. We got to arguing and I ended up leaving my purse on the fucking desk."

Piper felt bad for her girl, what kind of man steals from the woman that was trying to make life better for him? Trouble was selfish as fuck and she hated him. There was so much that Piper could tell her friend, but she didn't want to hurt her.

Trouble always took money out of their joint account, but Sutton didn't take that as stealing because he put money in that account too. He took more than he contributed, but some of his money was in there too. To blatantly take a wad of money that wasn't yours was something that Sutton wasn't willing to deal with.

"I can't believe that nigga took ya money but bitch if you don't go braid Kahleno up a bitch gone have to step on ya toes." She winked and the two laughed.

"Bitch I might have to fight you." Sutton pointed and the two fell out. "This nigga got the gift of gab, he will damn sure talk a bitch out her panties. His ass almost got me in that bathroom." Sutton threw her head in her hands like a school girl and giggled. Kahleno was bringing out things in her that she hadn't felt in years and as bad as she didn't want it to, it felt good. Then reality hit her. "What am I doing?"

"You're doing what's best for you, the fuck?" Piper's eyebrows bunched up and she turned up her lip. "You have got to stop letting that man bring you down to his level. I mean he's now stealing from you, what's next, him putting his hands on you?"

Sutton's head shot up and gave Piper the ugliest look. "Bitch you know better and so does he. One call to Hudson Chambers and everybody would be like Trouble who?"

"True, true!" Piper nodded her head in agreeance. "But still Sutton, he doesn't deserve you. Look at the bind he has you in."

"I'm not actually in a bind because I have the money but I'm not trying to go in my business account. I feel like once I start then I won't stop. And, if I got into my business account Hudson Chambers gone be on my ass because he's linked to it. I'm not trying to explain why I don't have the money to pay my house payment let alone why we're so behind."

Sutton's father was connected to her business accounts

which was another reason she refused to go in it. He kept a close eye on it to make sure that if something ever happened to him, she would be able to take care of herself.

"Sometimes love ain't enough Sutton." Sighing heavily Sutton looked her girl in the eye.

"I know Piper, I know." Looking at her watch she realized that she was way late for her appointment so she promised that she would catch up with Piper later. Walking back to the front like nothing happened. The shop was used to her and Trouble arguing but never involving another man. "Icelynn, I'm ready for you baby."

Icelynn looked up from her phone and made her way back to the chair. She unraveled her long platinum colored hair, that was perfectly dyed by Sutton. She smiled when she saw her because she knew what she was going through. Icelynn dealt with a man like Trouble before but her man was a little more ruthless. Which was what landed her in Charlotte.

"Hey boo, how are you?" she greeted Sutton with a hug.

"Going through but you know how that goes." Sutton chuckled but she knew all too well about how that went. "What we doing today?"

"I gotta dance tonight so let's do a high ponytail."

"We adding hair?"

"Nah, I don't want it in my way."

Icelynn was a stripper at Onyx strip club. She wasn't proud of her job, but she did what she had to do to take care of her daughter. She knew that being a stripper wasn't something that she wanted to do for the rest of her life which was why she was taking business management classes online and she was almost done with her degree.

"Heyyyy boo!" Piper hopped up on the chair and placed herself in Icelynn's lap. Icelynn giggled and shook her head. "You working tonight?"

"Yeah, y'all coming by? I can reserve a VIP." Sutton looked at Piper and they both looked at Icelynn.

"Hell yeah." They said at the same time.

"Cool I got you."

The rest of the day, Sutton worked nonstop. She was booked up until seven that night but that was normal for her on a Thursday night. Once she left the shop, she was dog tired, but she had all the energy she needed to cuss Trouble the fuck out. It was no surprise that he wasn't there. No use in wasting a good night. Sutton dressed to the nine and went to enjoy her free VIP table at Onyx to watch her girl do her thing.

CHAPTER FIVE

Indecent Proposal

Kahleno, his brothers, and his dad all sat around the bar in the warehouse that they had in the middle of town. No real business took place here this was more so where they had meetings and things like that.

"What's up with this girl son, tell me about her. You seem to really like her." Mega couldn't wait to question his son about the infamous Sutton, he would have when they left the salon, but he was bent out of shape about who her fiancé was.

"Who?" Cassidy asked and looked between Kahleno and his father. "I know you ain't talking about the girl from the party? You still hung up on that bitch?" Cassidy laughed but Kahleno and Mega cut their eyes at him.

"Yeah, I am and watch your fucking mouth!" Kahleno said as he grabbed the Cuban cigar from out of the ashtray and put it to his lips. He put fire to it and pulled. Cassidy chuckled and nodded his head. "I don't know what it is about her but from the first time I saw her I just felt something that I hadn't felt. Something was pulling me to her, and I couldn't ignore it. I mean pops the shit was crazy, I had for sure pussy sitting on my lap with about three on speed dial and I went home with a hard dick because shorty was a different breed and left my shit on brick."

AD was the first to laugh, if anyone knew his brother he did. Kahleno was the hoe of the family, he kept him a bad bitch around. The fact that he was sitting here trying to figure out why he was so attracted to this one girl who didn't even know who he was amused him.

"The bitch was fine as fuck though, her friend was too." Cassidy said nonchalantly.

"Watch ya mouth." Kahleno warned again and Cas threw his hands up in mock surrender. "This shit is weird as fuck pops but when I found out Trouble was her got damn fiancé, that shit pissed me off. He be wit Menz all the damn time and you know how that nigga get down and she don't deserve that. Shorty got her own business and she making her own money, she ain't got no kids, well at least I don't think."

"Nigga you don't even know if she got kids," AD interjected.

"I'll find all of that shit out tomorrow when I'm sitting between her legs while she braid my hair." Kahleno smiled big causing Cas and AD to laugh but his father's face remained neutral.

The room grew quiet because they all knew that when their father got like that, he was about to spit some knowledge on them or fill them in on some shit. They all gave him their undivided attention.

"When I met your mother, she was a quiet girl, she did hair out of her mother's house." My dad started to laugh. "She hated me I mean she haatteeeddd me. She always said she was not gonna be just another one of the girls." He smiled big. "But one day, we were at a party and I had three women with me but the minute she walked in the room, those three women didn't matter. I remember feeling my heart fluttering and feeling like a bitch." Again, he laughed but this time Kahleno joined in because he was feeling the same thing. "I didn't know a thing about this woman other than I wanted to be in her presence. So, I gave it all up for her and it was the best thing that I ever did." Mega looked down because he knew that he made a lot of mistakes when it came to Siya and he knew that he would take it all back if he could. "Son, if you feel as strongly for her as I think you do, despite not really knowing her go for it. But if you're not ready, leave her be until you are. Because the last thing you want to do is win her heart just to hurt her to the point where you lose her forever. So, get to know her but be careful how you move while you're trying to do that. Trust me. I messed up when I was with your mom, bad but she loved me through it." He dropped his head.

"You good pops?" Kahleno asked his father. He could tell that something was off with him, but he didn't want to pry.

"Yeah I'm good I'm just trying to let you know that sometimes sorry won't be enough so don't take that step if you ain't got on the right shoes."

"I feel you pops," Kahleno said taking in what his father had said.

He hadn't actually thought about it like that, all he knew was that he felt like he wanted to get to know her. The way she was with his son triggered something inside of him and he needed to see it through. What his father said was right, he could get to know her but don't go trying to lock her down before he was ready for that commitment.

Right now, his life was Kahlil, women and business. Could he see himself with just one woman and giving all of that up? He didn't know but if he could he had a feeling that Sutton would be the one. He smiled at the thought of her.

"The fuck you smiling at my nigga? That girl got you in the clouds and you ain't even hit yet," AD laughed at Cassidy's forwardness.

"Don't listen to them Kahleno, I used to do the same thing with your mother."

It was crazy to hear one of the most ruthless drug dealers to ever walk the streets talking about love like it's second nature. Mega always told his boys, to find that one woman that you can be vulnerable with and save that for her. No one else gets that but her that way when they're in the streets they don't feel the need to exert that energy anywhere else because they left it at home.

"I'm just messing with him." Cassidy said nodding at Kahleno.

"You my son are like your mother, you think the worst of everybody and your stubborn when it comes to love. I pray for the woman who falls for you." Mega chuckled and Cas shrugged with a grin on his face.

He knew it was true, he couldn't help it. Yes, he wanted to settle down, but he wouldn't settle for less either. The woman he wanted had to have a list of qualities and until he found that he would continue to do what he was accustomed to.

The warehouse doors opened and shut, everybody looked towards the door. When the visitors were in their sight Mega gave his son a knowing look. Biting down on his back teeth, Kahleno stood up and slipped his hands in his pocket. Something that he did to calm himself down.

Just looking at Trouble he knew that he didn't deserve Sutton, he knew what kind of man that Trouble was and the scowl on his face was pissing Kahleno off even more.

"You got my money?"

"No but I'm gone get it, here's $500 and if you give me a week, I'll get you everything I owe." Kahleno's tongue glided across the top row of his teeth, he was trying to work on his anger, but that shit was easier said than done.

He found it funny that this nigga brought him five hundred dollars after he had just given Sutton the same amount earlier that day. She wasn't that girl, there was no way that she was that girl. Disappointment filled his heart just that quick, he tried to shake it.

"Keep it, I'm tired of fucking with yo bitch ass." Cas stood up and started to approach Trouble who was now wringing his hands and unable to stay in one spot.

"Chill Cas." Kahleno stopped his brother who gritted his teeth and slipped his hands in his pocket. Cassidy was a no-nonsense type of dude and he wasn't with all the cat and mouse shit. You owed money then you either pay up or you get dealt with simple but Kahleno had another agenda. "Here's the deal you can pay the money or..."

"I'm gonna pay you your money," Trouble cut him off.

"Shut up!" Menz tried to warn him but before he could apologize, he had three nine millimeters pointed at his face. If he wasn't scared then, he damn sure was now. Making sure to make eye contact with each brother, silently begging for mercy.

"Don't ever in your fucking life cut me off again," Kahleno said through clenched teeth. "Now like I was saying pay the fucking money, die, or..." Kahleno lowered his gun as a sneaky grin appeared on his face. "You can grant me a weekend with your...*fiancée*." The room erupted into laughter, everyone except for Trouble. He didn't see the humor in what was being said, he actually found the shit disrespectful, even so there was nothing he could do about it and he knew it.

"I'll get you your money."

"Just imagine your slate wiped clean for just one weekend." As bad as Trouble wanted to shoot Kahleno in the face, he knew that he would never get away alive. Trouble cleared his throat and shook his head, there was no way the he would allow Sutton to be with another man. Especially a man like

Kahleno, he knew how he operated, and he would surely lose her.

"I'll get you your money!" Trouble's voice dripped with anger causing Kahleno to laugh.

"Alright then, I'll see you Friday." With his hands still in his pocket, Kahleno nodded his head. He watched as Menz said something to Trouble, "Menzell, and since you vouched for him, if he don't have my money, I'm making you kill him! So, make sure he gets it unless you want his blood on your hands."

Menz looked from his cousin to his friend, him and Trouble had grown close on the gambling scene and he thought of him like a brother. He didn't want to have to kill him. To be honest he could probably just give him the money, but he was too selfish for that. There was one way that he knew he could get Trouble the money and that was at the crap table.

Menz nodded his head and him and Trouble left as quickly as they came in. The minute they were out the door the Maler men shared a hearty laugh. Mega liked the way his son handled that situation; his wits had always been a highlight of his personality and he felt he got that from his father.

"Nigga did you really pull that indecent proposal bullshit?" Cas asked with a raised brow and a half smirk on his face. Without even looking at his brother he slowly nodded but he wasn't done. Kahleno was gonna push Troubles back against the wall to the point where he wouldn't have a choice but to offer up a weekend with Sutton.

Picking up his phone he placed a call, the phone rang a few times before a voice came on the line. "What up boss man?"

"Trouble and Menz are on their way. Let that nigga run up the numbers then take everything he's got!" A wicked some spread across Kahleno's face as he listened to Money run down his plan to him, after he was satisfied with everything, they said their goodbyes with promises to speak later on that night.

Slipping his phone back on his pocket he looked to his father and brothers, the amused looks on their faces brought a satisfactory one to his. "I hope she's worth it," AD said what Cassidy was thinking.

"Oh, she's worth it Adoree, I'm sure of it." Kahleno had never been so sure about anything in his life, which was crazy because all he knew was her name and that she owned a salon.

"Whatever, I'm going to Onyx." AD stood up and pulled up his Levi jeans that hung off of his waist. AD was taller than Kahleno yet shorter than Cas, he was the skinnier brother still weighed in at 240 pound of solid muscle. His athletic frame drew the women to him, but his emotionless demeanor and lack of communication often ran them away.

AD was a weird character, and it would take a special kind of woman to break through his hard exterior.

"Shit I'm riding too," Cas stood up too.

"Hell, I need a drink," Mega joined in and they all looked his way. He knew what they were all thinking, if Siya found out her husband was in a strip club then it would be hell to pay but right now he just needed to unwind. “What ya mama don’t know won’t hurt her.”

“For the record, I don’t want shit to do with this.” Kahleno threw his hands up.

“Pussy,” Mega joked with his son.

“Call me what you want pops but we ALL know how moms can be.”

“Who you telling?” Mega rubbed the spot where Siya had hit him with the flower pot the last argument they had before he got down here. Just thinking about how everything went down put him in a bad mood. “You know what, I’m just gonna go to the hotel and have a drink at the bar.” He looked to his sons who were all wearing smirks.

“Nah come on pops, what moms don’t know won’t hurt her,” Cassidy joked.

“Shut the hell up Cas, I swear something is wrong with you.” Mega laughed and excused himself. Making his way to the hotel, he was gonna try and call his wife and see if she was calm enough to talk to him.

CHAPTER SIX

Misconstrued

I was born to flex (Yes)..Diamonds on my neck...I like boardin' jets, I like mornin' sex (Woo!)...But nothing in this world that I like more than checks (Money)...All I really wanna see is the (Money)...I don't really need the D, I need the (Money)...All a bad bitch need is the (Money)...I got bands in the coupe (Coupe)... Bustin' out the roof...I got bands in the coupe (Coupe)...Touch me, I'll shoot (Bow)...Shake a little ass (Money).

Money by Cardi B blared through the speakers of Onyx night club. The energy was high, and everybody was having a good time. Piper was currently on the stage with the stripper who had her bent over and was dancing on her ass. She was throwing it back.

"Shake a little ass bitch!" Sutton yelled cheering her friend on.

The two had spent the majority of the night taking shots and vibing. Sutton was in the worst mood after realizing that Trouble had yet again put his gambling over her and their relationship. She often questioned herself as to why she kept allowing herself to go through the things that he kept putting her through, and the only answer she came up with is that she loved him.

Her mind subsequently traveled to Kahleno and she had to squeeze her legs together at the thought of him. A smile spread across her face, and she couldn't hold in the giggle that escaped her lips. She felt someone's eyes on her, but she did a quick scan of the room and no one was there that she noticed.

"Owwwww! That Cardi B shit go hard sis damn!" Piper wiped her forehead with the back of her hand. "Why you over here looking spaced out and shit?"

"Just thinking girl but fuck all that girl you were giving that stripper a run for her money." Sutton stuck her tongue out and high fived her friend.

"Okkkuuurrrrt! Shit I might have to hang up my color pallets and brushes and get down with the get down." The two burst out laughing as they grabbed a drink simultaneously and plopped down on the plush white sofa's that lined the free VIP area that Icelynn provided for them.

"Pipe what am I doing wrong?" Sutton finally said after a few minutes of silence between the two. "Like what the hell, I'm dope as fuck, pretty, sexy, got my shit together and don't need a nigga for shit. Why in the hell wouldn't he want to do right, why can't he just fucking do right?"

"Girl that shit ain't got nothing to do with you, that's all on him. You can be muthafuckin Michele Obama but if the nigga don't want to do right, he just ain't gone do right. He don't want to man up because he don't have to, you fix his fuck ups. Not intentionally but you do it."

"This time it's too much, not only did he spend up all of my got damn money for the mortgage, he took money out of my got damn pocketbook. What kind of man does that? He's supposed to be there to add to my life not take and take and take. I'm so sick of this shit and the bad part about all of it is he knows that I love him, and he uses that shit to his advantage."

"You know I love you," Piper slid over a little, so they were closer and didn't have to talk so loud over the music. "I would never tell you to leave him because that's not what friends do but I will say that you are too good for him. He doesn't deserve you Sut, at all. You have so much going for you and what does he have?" Piper looked at her friend with sympathetic eyes.

She knew that Sutton loved Trouble, why she didn't know but she did. Piper knew that Trouble was no good, and she had the proof.

"Excuse me." Both of the women looked up from the conversation and turned towards the deep baritone voice that was commanding their attention.

"Hi!" they both said at the same time.

"I'm Saque." Piper's eyes traveled from the top of his freshly cut hair to the brand-new J's on his feet. Her tongue inadvertently drug across her bottom lip right before she tucked it between her teeth. He chuckled at her forwardness but thought it was cute.

Saque had been across the room checking her out the entire time that she was on the stage with the stripper. He was out with his friends, they were celebrating him opening up his barber shop. Everyone was so proud of him for how he turned his life around. After catching an attempted murder charge on the strength of a cheating ex and serving 5 years, he knew he needed to get his life together. Living the street life got him in a world of trouble and he wasn't trying to go back there.

"Hey Saque, how are you? This is my girl Piper," Sutton said because Piper was clearly at a loss for words. She was so busy eye fucking him that her mind wouldn't focus on anything else and that included formulating words.

"Will you please tell your girl that I'm just as intrigued as she is and if she would talk to me then maybe would could get to know each other a little better, maybe even outside of this place." He winked at her and she smiled and cleared her throat.

"Sorry, I'm Piper."

"Aaaahhhh she speaks." When the corners of his mouth turned up into a smile, Piper almost melted where she sat. She saw hearts in her eyes, her heart was beating out of her chest and butterflies filled her stomach. She sighed lovingly.

"I will do anything you want me to do." She stuck her hand out and he accepted it. "God you're handsome."

"You lit the room, when you walked in, so I know how you feel. May I?" he held out his hand waiting for permission to join the VIP with the girls. Piper nodded her head while Sutton excused herself to head to the bathroom with hopes that Piper didn't move too fast with this man. Looking back, they were already cozy in the VIP, she shook her head and prayed that Mr. Saque was a good man.

On the other side of the club, AD had this real pretty red bone bent over his lap twerking on him like she needed her rent paid. She bounced her ass and grinded against his dick, he was standing at attention and had plans on taking her back to the private rooms and seeing if she could do the same thing naked.

Licking his lips, he went in a zone, AD loved strippers. It was something about the way they could move their body to a bad ass beat that drove him crazy. What they did was an art to him, that on top of the fact that they didn't require much. A few bands, a good nut and they were good.

"Damn bro, you gone fuck the bitch right here in front of us?" Cassidy said to the left of AD. "That pussy fat though, but she look like she stinks." He shrugged like he didn't just offend the woman that was dancing for his brother. She looked at Cassidy with the nastiest look right before she snatched away and collected her money to leave.

"What the fuck bro?" AD was pissed, he knew that he was going to be deep in Star's guts by the end of the night, but Cas had just fucked that up for him. He glared at his brother who wore a smirk and just shook his head before he burst out laughing.

"Yo you know how this nigga is, I don't even know why y'all let his ass come in this bitch," Kahleno said to the right of AD with a big booty chick in his lap putting on her best show. The more she danced the more he rained money down on her.

Whatever." Cassidy waved them off. "Y'all gone thank me one of these days."

Kahleno chuckled again as he tucked his lip between his teeth and the stripper twerked her ass all over his lap. He could feel someone watching him and when he looked up it was Lexus, he frowned at her and turned his attention back to the stripper.

Lexus didn't wait for an invitation as she made her way in the VIP with April and Menz in tow, making sure to give the stripper the nastiest look that she could muster up on her way to an empty seat.

"Sack chaser alert," Cassidy said loud enough to get a few stares from the other patrons that were close by.

"What is your problem?" April asked sliding in Menz's lap. Cassidy looked at her like she had lost her damn mind, she had no clue that she was so close to losing her life. She just kept looking at him waiting on him to answer her. Instead of addressing her he turned to Menz.

"If you don't want to see my fucking hogs gnawing at her fucking long ass neck, I suggest you teach her how and when not to speak."

April's eyes stretched, the knot in her throat grew to the size of a baseball and it was really hard to swallow it. She looked around for any kind of help and when her eyes landed on Menz she knew that she was by herself.

Kahleno tapped the stripper that was on his lap on the thigh for her to get up and she smacked her lips and collected the money that was around her feet. She just knew that she was gone get his sexy ass in a private room. The entire time she was dancing on him his dick was hard as a rock and she could tell that it was big. She made sure to throw the bitch that ruined her night a nasty look as she made her way out the VIP.

"Menz who in the fuck told you to bring them in my VIP?" Kahleno asked wiping off the invisible stuff on his pants, he stood up to adjust his dick that was hard as hell. Lexus' eyes went straight to the only part of him that she had the privilege to get to know.

"I was just— I saw y'all up here and I just wanted to hang with the family," he stumbled over his words.

"But do you see any bitches up here?" Kahleno tucked his hands in his pockets and glared at him. Mez shook his head.

Kahleno was about to address him again but something else caught his attention. Cassidy followed his eyes and landed on the women from the party. They were dancing and having a good ass time. When the next stripper, Ice was called to the stage, the two women went wild and started dancing along with the sounds of *Please Me* by Bruno Mars and Cardi B.

Cassidy watched as Piper rolled her hips around in a circle

while some nigga sat there with his tongue out. He shook his head because he had just had to school her about knowing her worth and he'd be damned if she didn't just bounce to another nigga further proving his point. He sat back in his seat, suddenly ready to go.

"You good bro?" Kahleno asked with a smirk on his face.

"Fuck you nigga."

Kahleno saw exactly what his brother was looking at and he didn't blame him. Both of the women were fine as hell and had bodies that women paid for. He understood his attraction, he also knew that Cassidy was too stubborn to act on it. She had been with his cousin, so his ego was definitely getting in the way.

Sutton and Piper were cheering their girl on as she did her thing, Icelynn was very talented with her body. It was like she went off into another world and didn't even realize all of those people were watching her. They both were in awe every time they watched her dance.

The Tom Ford Cologne assaulted her nostrils and the butterflies made their way into her stomach before he even stepped up behind her.

"So, you just gone give that nigga money that I gave you?" was the first thing out of Kahleno's mouth. Even though he wanted to say so much more, he felt like he needed to get that off of his chest. He couldn't pursue her if her loyalty was with him on the level that she supported his gambling. "I didn't take you as that kind."

Sutton swung around, the nerve of him speaking on something that he knew nothing about. He didn't know what the hell she was going through with Trouble and for him to speak on it pissed her off.

"You don't know what the hell you're talking about." The tremble in her voice let him know what he needed to know. He slowly backed away from her and made his way back over to where he had just come from.

Sutton watched his back the entire time, very confused as to what the hell happened. Then it hit her, he must have took the money that he stole from her and tried to pay on his debt. She shook her head and the tears that were threatening to fall, spilled from her eyes.

Piper embraced her friend as she cried on her shoulder. She understood what she was going through and she hated Trouble for putting her through it. As bad as she wanted to just yell to the roof top for her to leave him, she couldn't do that, she knew that Sutton didn't need that. Sometimes people don't need you to try and fix the problem, sometimes they just need you to listen and be there and that's what Piper thought Sutton needed right now.

"I'm really starting to hate him Piper!"

"I know, you ready to go?" she looked at her friend and she shook her head. Icelynn had just finished her set and she saw Sutton get upset. Those two were the only two that had made her feel welcomed when she moved to Charlotte. She considered them friends and wanted to make sure they were okay.

"Hey y'all leaving already?" Icelynn asked when she got to the girls.

"Yeah, even when Trouble ain't here, he's here." Sutton rolled her eyes. "I think I'm done with him though. I really am, sometimes love ain't enough you know?" She shrugged her shoulders.

She didn't know if it was from the embarrassment or just everything coming at once but her and Trouble's time was coming to an end and soon. Her friends comforted her while she got herself together.

Piper and Saque exchanged numbers and promised to go out the following week. They told Icelynn bye and headed for the door. When they got close to the brothers' section Sutton looked over and shook her head when she saw Lexus in Kahleno's lap.

She wasn't sure why that pissed her off, but it did, and she wasn't the one to hold her tongue. Strutting in the section with her best walk, she gained the attention of every man in the section, especially Kahleno.

His tongue damn near fell out of his mouth as he focused on the gap between her legs. Her hips spread just enough to see her ass from the back and the black leggings that she had on made it stick out just a little more.

"Damn she got a fat ass," was heard from beside the section. Kahleno bit down on his back teeth, getting pissed all over again.

"For the record, that money was stolen from me." She pointed her finger in her chest and made Kahleno feel like shit. He went to move Lexus so he could talk to her. "Nah playa, you straight enjoy you night and I would prefer you stay the hell away from me and my shop. I don't have time for the bullshit, I get enough of that at home." She raised a brow and turn to walk out of the section and out the door with Piper.

"I know y'all better stop looking at her got damn ass," Kahleno said through gritted teeth. "Disrespectful mutha-fuckas." Cassidy chuckled and shrugged his shoulders.

"Bro you fucking up, baby girl sexy as hell."

"Yo that's my dude Trouble's wife," Menz spoke up and Kahleno shot him a look.

"Do it look like I give a fuck about any of that? He gone be hog food if he don't get me my money and then his ass won't even be an issue any longer." Kahleno grilled him.

"Piper was looking good as hell too; her short ass can get it," Cassidy said glaring at Menz.

"That's fucked up cuz." Menz shook his head causing April to swing around daring him to continue his statement.

"Fuck you nigga, keep talking reckless and you gone get ya ass beat again. You wanted that bop head bitch on ya lap. Piper free game homeboy." Cassidy laughed.

Kahleno's mind went to Sutton and the fact that she said that Trouble stole from her. She might have said for him to stay away from her but now he wanted her more than ever. Something in him wanted to save her from Trouble and his bullshit.

CHAPTER SEVEN

Behind her back

"Yes Trouble, right there baby," Sunny moaned as Trouble moved in and out of her. He needed a stress reliever after the shit that he had just done. He knew that when Sutton saw him, she was going to tear him a new one so going home wasn't an option for him right now. So here he was.

Pressing one of her legs all the way to the bed and then holding the other straight up, Trouble watched as his dick slid in and out of her. Besides Sutton, Sunny had the best pussy out of any of the girls he was fucking.

"This pussy good as fuck Sunny."

"All for you daddy." She coached him, she wanted to feel every inch that Sutton talked about during their girl's night in at the shop. The detail that Sutton went into piqued her interest and she went for it. "Show me how much you love me."

Trouble grunted and bit his lip, there was no love in his heart for Sunny. He loved Sutton and that would never change. He just felt like she acted like she was better than him and it kept him doing something stupid.

Troubled lowered himself and kissed her nice and slow to keep her from talking. Gripping both of her legs in the crease of his arm he held her close as he stroked her like it meant something.

"Fuck girl."

"Damn baby I feel it in my stomach, shit you gone make me cum!" Sunny yelled out.

"Shut up girl before you wake up the damn kids." Trouble hissed in her ear and then latched onto her perfect nipples and sucked lightly. He was trying to make her cum so he could. She was always doing the most.

"Yes, baby right, fuck yes right there. Go deeper!" he did as he was told and in no time, she was coating his dick and he was shooting up her walls. They were never careful, and Trouble didn't even think twice about it.

"Damn girl," he panted as he rolled off of her and on to his back. He placed his arm over his eyes and then other across his stomach. "You on birth control, right?" he asked her peeking from under his arm.

"Yeah!" she didn't sound convincing, but he didn't have the energy to fight her on it.

All of his problems came rushing back to his mind just

that quick, that session didn't help as much as he thought it would. Not only did he steal the money from her, he went to the casino and played the money won big and instead of taking the money and leaving, he got greedy and blew it all back.

Sutton was going to kill him. He hated that he had been on a losing streak lately and he didn't know how to come out of it. Now he had to come up with 20 g's or give her to Kahleno for a weekend.

His stomach turned at just the thought of having to tell the woman he loved that he offered her up to clear his debt, but the way it was looking he wouldn't have a choice. The days were closing in on him and he couldn't see a way out of it.

"What got you so quiet?" Sunny asked. When her and Trouble hooked up it was usually a good time filled with laughs and sex but today, he seemed so disconnected. "Must have something to do with Sutton and Kahleno."

He lifted up and glared at her, she knew every fucking thing about everybody. That's why she didn't have friends, she was always starting some shit and minding other people's business. Her own damn sister didn't even fuck with her like that because of the shit she did to her.

"You don't know what the fuck you talking about so let that shit go. Sutton ain't going nowhere but at home, in our damn bed." Hatred dripped from the words leaving his mouth causing Sunny to scoff.

"Well they looked cozy at the strip club." She laughed and

he jumped up and started putting his clothes on. "Wait where you goin?"

"I'm tired of your fucking mouth, I'm sick of you always talking about shit, just learn to shut the fuck up sometimes and maybe you won't be by your got damn self. Ever thought about that shit Sunny? Half the shit you be saying don't even be true because you just repeating what the nosey bitches tell you at the shop. That shit is so unattractive."

"So is owing the fucking Maler brothers over fifty thousand dollars," she sassed back.

Trouble took a few deep breaths and tried to calm his nerves, but it wasn't working. He was two seconds from wrapping his hands around her throat and squeezing. Shaking his head, he walked towards the door about to leave but she kept going.

"Yeah and everybody know you fucking Cami too. I wonder what your precious Sutton would do if she found out just how much of an ain't shit nigga you are." She was on her knees antagonizing him.

Without thinking Trouble backhanded the fuck out of Sunny, sending her flying back off the bed and hitting her head. She jumped up ready to swing.

"Yo if you hit me Ima beat yo ass like you was a nigga. I suggest you calm the fuck down." he pointed at her and she stopped in her tracks. She was starting to see why Sutton was after Kahleno, Trouble wasn't shit and she knew that if she hit him back that he would hold true to his word.

"When I come out of this bathroom you better have your

ass out of my house and don't ever fucking come back." she walked to the bathroom in her room and slammed the door.

Trouble was just fucking up every which way and he was falling deeper and deeper into shit. Soon it was going to be over his head and there was going to be nothing that he could do about it. He turned to leave but Sunny's purse caught his eyes before he did, he ran to the dresser and opened her pocket book. When his eyes fell on her wallet, he opened it and his eyes lit up.

Sunny was a hair stylist just like Sutton and most of her clients paid with cash so she had a lot of cash for a full day of sew ins and weave. Trouble slid the money out of her wallet and placed the wallet back how he found it and made his way out of her room and her house as fast as he could.

When he got to his car, he counted the money and had close to twelve hundred dollars. A smile spread across his face as he picked up his phone and called Menz. He had to make something shake and fast.

CHAPTER EIGHT

I'm ready when you are

"I have a delivery for Sutton Chambers," The *Pro Flowers* guy said as he made his way into the room full of beautiful women. He suddenly became self-conscious as everyone in the room turned his way. Sutton chuckled.

"I'm Sutton." She made her way to the front of the shop wiping her hands on her apron. She smiled at the delivery guy and she couldn't help but blush under his stare because he didn't try to hide the fact that he was checking her out.

Sutton was the most beautiful woman that he had ever seen, he couldn't help but stare at her. When she touched his hand to get his attention, he felt something spark inside of him and he knew he had to have her.

"Oh, I'm sorry, sign right here beautiful." He said and all

the women in the shop began their chatter. Sutton shook her head and signed where she was told to sign. She took her what looked like three dozen roses and turned to walk away after telling him thank you. "Damn." He muttered to himself as he made his way out the door.

"Dang Sutton, you be getting all the men." Pebbles, another stylist in the salon said and then started to laugh. Pebbles loved Sutton, she knew her when she was a little girl. She used to be friends with her mother, so she felt the need to look out for her and that included her hating Trouble just like everyone else.

"Who, the delivery guy? He's harmless." She giggled.

"Awww shit who got flowers?" Piper said coming from the back.

"Why do you have to be so loud child?" Pebbles said glaring at Piper.

"Auntie P don't start with me, now I even brought you a plate today because I cooked that cabbage that you like and you still fussing at me."

"Me eating your food ain't got nothing to do with me eating your food, but where my plate at?" Sutton giggled at the exchanged. They stayed into it because Pebbles looked at herself like an auntie to the girls and she tried to spread wisdom whenever they would listen.

"Umhmmm, it's in the fridge. I want my Tupperware back too."

"When I get mine back, you'll get yours back." She said in

a hushed tone, but we still heard her. Piper shook her head and laughed. Turning her attention to Sutton, Piper looked down at the card that was hanging from the flowers.

"Ahh that's mine, thank you very much." Sutton snatched the card from her and opened it up. Her eyes scanned the words on the card and tears pooled at the rim of her eyes. She hadn't seen Trouble since the day that he stole the money from her and that was almost a week ago. Her heart had come to grips with them being over, she even went as far as changing the locks to her house.

Now here he was laying his heart on the line while she was working on closing hers. Tears fell rapidly down her face as she dropped the card on her station and excused herself for just a minute. Piper picked up the card and read its contents...

My wife,

My life is all fucked up right now and I hate myself for letting it get so bad that it came in between the two of us. My love for you has never changed and I hope your heart still beats for me too. It kills me that our relationship took the biggest hit of all. I'm gonna get out of this shit but I need you by my side. I will do whatever I have to do to make this right baby just give me the chance. I need you in my life baby. I love you.

Your Future Husband

Piper's eyes teared up as she looked in the direction of her friend. She felt so bad for Sutton because she knew deep down that she loved Trouble, but he was no good for her. She just hoped that she didn't fall for his shit this go round. Her friend deserves the world and she knew he couldn't give it to her.

"Let me see this shit." Pebbles said as she read over the card and then looked up just in time to see Sutton rejoining them. Sutton walked over to Pebbles and took the card from her and slid it into her station. Pebbles shook her head because she knew that meant that more than likely she would be accepting his request.

Sighing, Pebbles went back to her station and made the decision to call Hudson. She tried to stay out of Sutton's business as much as she could, but she promised her mother that she would take care of the both of them if something ever happened to her and that's what she was going to do.

"Sut you good?" Piper asked and she nodded her head and wiped a lone tear that slid down her face. She shook her head and grabbed another pre-threaded needle and went back to work on the full sew in that she was on.

"My bad girl," she told her client. "These niggas be stressful."

"I already know." She giggled and went back to her phone. She was busy telling her best friend about this guy she met, his name was Spiff and he was connected to the Maler men.

She was secretly hoping that he was different, but she guessed she'd just have to see.

Sutton worked on the girl's head as she drifted into her thoughts. She hated that Trouble made her feel this way, she was so conflicted in how she felt that it almost made her feel crazy. On one hand she knew that he would never change, if he hadn't changed by now, he never would.

The on the other hand she knew that she loved him but was love really enough to keep going through this shit. It was only a matter of time before his gambling caught up to him and put her in the cross fire.

Her mom would be so disappointed in her, her mom always said that if a man shows you who he really is, and you don't believe him that makes you the fool. Right now, Sutton felt like a fool. She wanted to talk to her father so bad, but she knew that once she did, her relationship with Trouble would definitely be over so she needed to make sure that's what she wanted before she made that step.

As the day went on, Sutton sulked more and more into her feelings. All she wanted to do was to sit at home, drink some wine and try and figure out her life. The next person that walked through the door was sure to alter that in a matter of minutes.

Per usual, his cologne filled her nostrils before she even saw his face. Rolling her eyes in the back of her head Sutton knew that she was not in the mood to deal with his shit. She was still pissed at the fact that he played her with the same girl from the barn. She didn't know why she was mad she didn't know anything about this man. Except for the fact he was fine as fuck and she had an unexplainable attraction to him, one that she couldn't shake when he was in her presence.

"We're closed," Sutton said drawing a chuckle from Kahleno.

He knew that she was pissed but he also knew that she was drawn to him just like he was to her. After that night at the strip club he showed up to get his hair done and the shop was dark as ever. He decided to give her a minute, but that shit was over, and he was here to claim what was sure to be his.

"You flaked on me." he said sitting in her chair ignoring her objections.

"Kahleno I've got appointments. I don't have time for your bullshit."

"Who's next?" He said and looked at the ladies that were sitting in the waiting area. A dark-skinned chick raised her hand like she was in school, indicating that it was her turn to get her hair done. "I'll give you a g to let me get your appointment."

The girl's eyes stretched as wide as they could go, she lived paycheck to paycheck. She only came to Sutton once a month because that's all she could afford. That thousand dollars would put her ahead in her bills.

"Girl you do not have to do that." Sutton waved her over at the same time Kahleno pulled out a wad of money and peeled off ten one hundred-dollar bills. The girl looked back and forth between the two of the them and headed in their direction. When she got there, she looked at Sutton.

"Sorry girl, a bitch can do a lot with a G. Can I reschedule next week?" Sutton grilled the girl who shrugged her shoulders. She couldn't be mad at her because she understood where she was coming from.

"I got you," Sutton said nodding her head and went to the back to get a few towels and other things that she would need to wash and braid his hair.

Bending down to grab the grease off the bottom of the shelf she felt something hard pressed against her ass. Lifting up she tried to turn around, but he snaked his arms around her waist and held her there.

"You can't tell me that this doesn't feel good," he whispered in her ear. "I know we don't know each other, and it may be hard for you to see it now, but this is right. Me and you are meant to be."

"I don't even know you."

"Small things, simple things that could be fixed if you let me." He kissed the side of her cheek and then let his lips linger for just a second. A cold chill traveled down her back and she shivered.

Kahleno smiled to himself and then he turned to go back to the front of the salon and regain his seat in her chair. All the women in attendance was damn near drooling over him, regardless of the fact he was there for Sutton.

"Mr., I don't know who you are but if you hurt my baby, I'ma have to fuck you up," Pebbles said never looking up from her client's head. Kahleno didn't take the threat too seriously, he was actually glad to see someone had her back other than Piper. He nodded his head but opted not to say nothing.

Sutton was still in the back trying to get herself together. Kahleno was the only person who could take her there even if she didn't want to go. Not even Trouble could reach the depths that Kahleno had and they hadn't even had a real conversation. Sutton was in trouble and she knew it.

"What are we doing?" she asked him lowly.

"I'm about to get in your heart and shake your world up and you don't even know it yet. That's what the fuck we're doing," he said with so much conviction it sent another cold chill down her neck.

Blood rushed to her face making it warm, she knew that her cheeks were a rosy color. Pebbles looked at her and could see how smitten she was with the young man that commended everyone's attention. She knew who Kahleno was and she also knew that Hudson wouldn't approve. She sighed heavily and decided to mind her business for now.

"Kahleno I was talking about your hair."

"Oh, I want it cut like Kahlil's but keep it long on the top." Sutton was shocked, she ran her hands through his hair. She loved the feel of his curls going through her fingers, it was somewhat therapeutic. "Yo you starting something," he said and placed his hand over his now visible hard on causing Sutton to pull her hands back and cover her mouth, releasing a giggle. "It's not funny man." He spun around so that they were facing each other.

"I didn't even do anything." She whined.

"A simple touch from you excites me, your smile excites me, the way you smell excites me so technically you do everything. Right now, you rubbing through my hair was taking me to a place that could get you into a lot of trouble."

Sutton's nipples hardened and protruded out of the thin V-neck Nike shirt that she had on. She had to remember to stop wearing sports bras to work but it fit her laid-back attire today. Kahleno's eyes focused on hers, his stare was so intense that she had to shy away. Sutton had to place her hand over her heart to keep it from beating out of her chest.

What the fuck is wrong with you Sutton, get your shit together. She coached herself. Clearing her throat, she turned him so that he was facing the opposite direction. She threw her head back and took in a deep breath, she could feel his eyes on her, but she knew that she had turned the chair around. When she looked up, she was staring at the mirror that lined the wall that he was facing, and he was staring directly at her. He was definitely making this hard and she couldn't help the feelings that he was giving her.

"W—what made you want to cut your hair?" she stammered, clearing her throat again.

"I make you nervous, you can't even formulate sentences when I'm in your presence." The half smirk on his face made Sutton want to slap the shit out of him and shove her tongue down his throat at the same damn time. "You can't control yourself around me and I like that, it lets me know that it's real. That you're real and just so you know." He leaned further up in the seat, so he was closer to the mirror, Sutton looked on with anticipation. "I want you just as bad." With that he sat back in his seat and crossed his arms across his chest.

The two competed in a staring competition until Pebbles cleared her throat and the two of them looked her way. She nodded to the waiting area and every woman in there was watching, hanging on to every word, every interaction just waiting for what would happen next.

Sutton smiled at the nosey women and started moving her hands through his hair again. Then she remembered what he said so she drew her hand back suddenly and then glanced in the mirror. Kahleno thought that was the funniest thing in the world, even though Sutton wasn't amused.

"Aight man chill, I'ma stop fucking with you for now." Again, he smirked. "Kahlil asked me to cut my hair like his so we could be twins and you know I can't tell my little man no."

"Awwwwww," came from the waiting area, the women were all wanting to know what the deal was between her and Kahleno. If she wasn't trying to bag him then a few of them would have loved to take her place.

"Y'all nosey ass ain't got no shame." Pebbles said drawing a few lip smacks and eye rolls. "Yeah whatever, he don't want nothing to do with y'all so just mind ya damn business." She was so protective when it came to Sutton and she hated to feel like someone was out to get her.

"How's my little boyfriend doing?" Sutton smiled, she

really had taken to the little man in the short time that they spent together.

"Bad as fuck, with his cussing ass."

"I wonder where he gets it from Kahleno," she grabbed his hair and pulled him back a little so that he was looking at her. He drug his tongue across his bottom lip and tucked his lip between his teeth. It was that moment that Sutton knew that she had made a mistake. Shaking her head, she released his hair and then started to comb it, ignoring the look that he was giving her. "I'm serious Kahleno, you have to watch what you say around him. His mind is like a sponge, what the hell does he know about *rabid hoes?*"

Kahleno covered his mouth with his fist and laughed at Suttons attempt to copy what Kahlil said to Sunny the day he came in the shop. He knew what she was saying was true it was just hard as hell to catch himself sometimes. Sutton narrowed her eyes in the mirror and then grabbed the clippers.

"Aight step mama, I got you. I will be more cautious of what comes out of my mouth on the strength of our son." Sutton didn't bother to say anything she just shook her head and began to cut his hair the exact same way that he cut Kahlil's.

The whole time she moved around with the clippers and the scissors, Kahleno watched her. He could tell that she loved what she did because not once did the smile ever leave her face while she was working. He would have liked to have had something to do with that, but he knew it was merely the fact that she loved her craft and he respected it.

"What's your favorite color?" Kahleno asked out of the blue.

"Huh?"

"You heard me, what's your favorite color?"

"Pink, all shades of pink." She smiled and looked around, he followed her eyes and realized the shop had a soft pink and gold color scheme. The sinks were rose gold and so were the picture frames. He nodded his head and smiled.

"What's your favorite food?"

"What you trying to do Kahleno?"

"I'm trying to get to know the woman that I'll spend the rest of my life with. Now if you would just answer the question and stop stalling, we can get this over with. Then maybe we can get to the good part." He smirked and Sutton could feel the moistness of her panties.

"Seafood, I love seafood." She gave into his conversation and she must say that for the rest of the time she cut and washed his hair she enjoyed their conversation. They got to know a lot about each other in that short amount of time. "So, what do you do for a living? I see the suits and besides the other night all I see you in are these fly ass suits."

"You think I'm fly?"

"Answer the question Kahleno, I thought you wanted to get to the good stuff." Sutton regretted the words the minute they were out of her mouth. He spun around, grabbed her by the waist and placed her in his lap. His hard on was poking her thigh begging to find a place to call home.

"You can't play with me like that." He said to her seriously. "I want you so fucking bad that it feels like my dick could burst right now. Seeing you in your element does something to me, so unless you want to take a trip to your office, I suggest you chill with the slick comments."

"Oh, you can say slick shit, but I can't?" Sutton said purposely sliding back into his lap. She was playing a dangerous game and she knew it, but she was starting to feel like things with her and Trouble was over. Despite his attempt to get her attention with the flowers she still felt like they weren't meant to be, that maybe what they had sailed a while ago.

"I can and will back up my slick shit, can you say the same?" he tilted his head to the side, and she smiled and relaxed in his arms.

It felt good to feel truly wanted, it probably wasn't a good idea for her to be all laid up with a man and she hadn't properly ended it with the man that she already had. Sighing at her reality. "You never answered my question sir." She said needing to get up but not wanting to.

"Ever heard of Maler farms?" he said, and Sutton nodded her head. That was the biggest meat market on this side of the US, everyone knew who they were and what they provided. "I'm Kahleno Maler."

Sutton's eyes grew the size of saucers, causing Kahleno to laugh. "You're lying."

"No, I'm not, what I got to lie for. That's why I asked you if you knew who I was the first night we met." Sutton went back to the night at the barn and it all started coming together.

"I am going to kill Piper."

"It's cool that you didn't know who I was, I liked that. It was weird as fuck, but I was definitely intrigued. I think it will makes shit that much better." He smiled and she joined in.

"Alright playa, what ya think?" She spun him around and faced the mirror. Moving his hands down the sides of his head. He couldn't believe that he let Kahlil talk him into cutting his hair, but he must admit that it was dope.

"So, when you gone braid the top?" he asked looking at his watch. He had some business to attend to shortly and it couldn't be missed.

"Just let me know when you're ready." Sutton said, she had actually enjoyed herself today. Their conversation was effortless, and she found herself getting lost in his presence so much so that she slowed down the process of finishing his hair.

He kept her mind off of her shit with Trouble and she welcomed that. Too bad that she knew it wouldn't last long. Kahleno grabbed her thighs with his massive hands and squeezed just a bit causing her to shiver.

"I'm ready when you are, and I mean that in every way imaginable." He smiled and stood up directly in front of her so that his chest brushed against her breast. The feel of her hardened nipples made his dick harder than it already was. "Fuck!" he said under his breath.

"Kahleno—" Sutton started but was stopped by Kahleno crashing his lips against hers, parting them with his tongue and invading her mouth. Grabbing the back of her head he deepened the kiss.

At first Sutton was caught off guard, so she just stood there and let him do whatever. Then just like the night at the barn something took over her and she grabbed the sides of his face and joined in the passion filled kiss that had everyone's attention, even Pebbles.

"Damn y'all gone come up for air?" She said causing the shop to erupt into laughter.

Sutton finally pulled back with a huge smile on her face and rested her forehead on his chest. Kissing the top of her head he pulled her closer to him and held on to her for what felt like forever before lifting her chin and kissing her lips one more time.

"Give me your phone," he demanded and without any push back she reached in the pocket of her Nike joggers and handed him her phone. He turned it back towards her, she brought her face into view and the phone opened. He pressed a few buttons and then glared up at her. "That nigga ain't yo fucking husband."

"Well Kahleno he was supposed to be." She said shyly.

"Fuck all that." Waving her off he pressed a few more buttons and then called his phone so that he had her number too. Handing her back her phone, he kissed her again and whispered in her ear. “I can get use to those lips, I’ll call you later.” Kissing her one more time Kahleno went into his pocket and pulled out a wad of money. Without even counting it he placed it in her hand and turned to head out the door before she could object.

Sutton could feel all eyes on her, instead of giving them what they wanted she turned and made a beeline to her office where she fell in her chair and grabbed her chest.

“Ahhhh!” she said. She was stuck and seeing hearts and stars and shit. That school girl feeling came over her and she couldn’t control the giggles that came soon after. Kahleno had her head in the clouds, and she didn’t know if she could come down from that.

The door to her office opened and shut. She was on such a high that she didn’t want to look at who had just walked in, in fear that they would ruin it. Pebbles didn’t give her a choice though because the next words out of her mouth turned Sutton’s world upside down.

“Do you know what you’re getting yourself into young lady?” Sutton finally opened her eyes and gave Pebbles the attention that she was demanding. “Do you know that him and his brothers not only supply Charlotte with meat, they also supply the whole city of Charlotte with the best coke anyone has ever seen?”

Sutton felt her chest cave in and all of a sudden, she couldn’t breathe. How could someone so perfect be a drug dealer. She didn’t care one way or another personally, because

Kahleno seemed like the kind of man that would protect you with his life, but she knew that her dad would never approve.

"Whyyyy?" Sutton grabbed the sides of her head before she lowered it. "Don't I deserve to be happy?

"Baby I'm just looking out for you. This is your life, I just want you to be careful."

CHAPTER NINE

D***addy's girl***

"Ms. Chambers, very nice to see you. It's always a good day when you get to see two Chambers in one day," Lisa, the bank representative said to Sutton as she walked into her office. The confusion on her face must have registered because she held up her hand and clicked a few buttons on the computer. "You dad came by and made the late payment on your mortgage."

"He did what?" Sutton's palms became sweaty as she thought about the conversation that she was going to have to have with her father. He was going to tear her a new one and she knew it.

"Yeah, he came in this morning, we tried to call you the other day and didn't get an answer. We called the secondary number which was Braxton and—"

"That number no longer applies, you can just delete it. We are no longer living together at the moment." *And depending on what you say next we may be over forever.* Sutton thought to herself.

"Okay I'll do that now, but he instructed us to call your father to make the payment. He was next on our list to call anyway if we couldn't reach you again, so I called him, and he came right down. He's on all of your financial information anyway so legally I did what I had to do."

She wasn't mad at Lisa for doing what she had to do because Sutton felt like she should have been grown about the situation and let them know what was going on instead of dodging their calls. This was her fault and her fault alone.

"It's fine," Sutton stood to leave but then thought about her situation and decided to fix it while she was there.

"Would you like us to link your business account to your main account and that way if something like this ever happens then we can just take it from there."

"First thing I need to do is close the account with Braxton, then I would like to open up a personal account and link my business account." She nodded her head and got to work.

Mentally preparing herself to deal with her dad was hard. Sutton never knew if he was going to be the kind loving father or the enforcer, laying down the law. He was a Gemini, and she truly believed that there was two of him.

"Good morning Sutton, your dad has been waiting for you all morning." His receptionist, Rachel said.

"Really?"

"Yeah, I'll buzz you right back."

The closer Sutton got to the hallway, the thicker the air became. The sweat on her brow was starting to trickle down her forehead. She wiped her forehead with the back of her hand as she slowly opened the door to her father's office.

He was sitting in the chair with his back to her, when he turned around he had the phone to his ear and Sutton didn't miss the smile that donned his handsome face. When he saw her, he abruptly hung up the phone and gave her his attention.

"Who was that?" Sutton didn't know how she felt about her dad dating, even though it was none of her business she still wasn't happy about it. Her mom should have been the only woman in his heart even though she had been gone for many years.

"No one, come in and sit down."

"Oh we're lying to each other now?" Sutton's hands found her hips as she felt her anger get to her. Looking into her dad's eyes, she saw them turning darker and his shoulders tense up and then he sighed trying to calm himself down.

"I don't know Sutton, are we lying to each other?" It was his turn to give her attitude which diminished hers instantly.

"Listen daddy—"

"No, you listen, what the hell is going on Sutton and don't you lie to me. Why in the hell were you four damn months behind on your mortgage? Why would you let things get that far out of hand when you know that you could have just come to me?"

"Because I didn't want you to think that I can't handle myself and I didn't want you to know that..."

"That Trouble is a piece of shit like I told you when you introduced me to the little fucker. When I see him I'ma wrap my fucking hands around his neck and squeeze until his little beady ass eyes pop out." Hudson gritted.

He knew that he didn't like Trouble from the first time he laid eyes on him. He warned him about how he felt about his daughter when he asked to marry Sutton. Hudson didn't play when it came to his daughter and everyone knew that.

This nigga must take me as a joke, Hudson said to himself. He fought hard to keep Maniac, his street name, in the cage but the thought of his daughter being mistreated in any way brought something ugly out of him.

"See daddy that's why I didn't want to tell you, I knew you would take it overboard. You're a hot head and you been itching to get to Trouble."

"What kind of man allows his woman to get in a bind like that? I bet he was gambling too, wasn't he?" Sutton didn't answer she just put her head down, Hudson released an evil chuckle. "I didn't raise you to deal with shit like that Sutton and you know it."

"I know daddy, but he wasn't always like this, in the beginning he was everything that I ever wanted in a man. He took care of me, even though I didn't need him to, but he was supportive. He was a good dude and I fell in love with him. When shit started going downhill, I was too far in."

"That is no excuse, being too far in." Hudson shook his

head. "Fuck that, when that nigga started spending your money that's when you were supposed to cut him off. He don't even contribute to your life Sutton. How long as this been going on? This is worse than you dating some drug dealer!" Hudson fumed.

"What difference does it make? I've reached my breaking point and I'm going to meet with him later today to break things off with him."

"Oh, so it's been going on that long?" Hudson raised a brow

"Daddddyyyyy!" she whined.

"Don't daddy me, I'm pissed the hell off, and you know it. I taught you better than that Sutton. Don't let anyone take you down, if you go down..."

"Go down on my own terms!" she finished his sentence. "Yeah daddy I know. I mean you act like he was out here cheating on me and hitting on me. I needed to see the lesson in this, and I did, and I'm done." She threw her hands up and Hudson sighed.

He knew that his daughter was right, she needed to go through life lessons to prepare her for life if something ever happened to him. He also felt the need to be there for her and protect her from all the bullshit that life had to offer.

Sutton was raised right, she was spoiled but her foundation was strong. He knew that she would be able to take care of herself no doubt, but he also knew how men could be, he knew how he was. He gave her a sympathetic look and got up from his chair. Making his way around to where she was sitting, he wrapped his hands around her and hugged her.

"I love you baby girl."

"I love you too daddy."

"I just want whatever man you end up with to treat you right, you don't deserve anything less."

"I know daddy, I promise it'll be okay..." She smiled at her father. "That's how I knew you had paid my mortgage because I went to pay it and close the joint account that we had together. I opened my own personal account and joined my business account. Love won't get me again daddy, I promise."

Hudson chuckled, he knew that it was a lie, but he would be sure to be there for his daughter if she ever needed him. He knew that Sutton was a hopeless romantic and she would do anything to have the type of relationship that he had with his wife. She had expressed on more than one occasion that she wanted what they had.

"Well if you need me you know I'm here."

"I know daddy and I love you." She looked down at her watch, she had an appointment that she couldn't miss so she kissed her dad and made her way out of his office and to her shop that was just five minutes away.

Walking into the shop, Sunny gave her the look of death and she had no clue why. Little did Sutton know, Sunny had slept with Trouble on numerous occasions and now she was pregnant. Not only that, Trouble stole all of her money for her kids back to school stuff.

"Do you have an issue?" Sutton asked with her hand on her hips. Sunny rolled her eyes and called her next client.

As bad as Sutton wanted to address her, she didn't, her conversation with her dad played over and over in her mind. She knew that her dad raised her better than what she was accepting. Trouble wasn't the man for her, and she was starting to see that. She loved him but sometimes love just wasn't enough.

CHAPTER TEN

H*ere we go*

"Where's he at?" Kahleno said the minute Karson had the door open, she had called him earlier and told him that she had to take Kahlil to the doctor. When she found out he had the flu she called and let Kahleno know.

He felt horrible that he didn't come when she called him the first time. Karson was a nurse and she overreacted about everything, her favorite line was *it's better to be proactive.* So, every little cough and sneeze needed to be checked.

Kahleno wasn't complaining he just didn't know when to jump at her calls or when to play the background. Today was one of those days he should have went to see about his son.

"He's in his room. He asked if you could stay. I told him he would have to ask you." She said to Kahleno's back as he made his way to the back. It broke his heart to see his little man down.

"Aye man you good?" Kahleno leaned against the door frame.

"Nah pops, pimp down, pimp in distress," Kahlil said making Kahleno laugh. Making his way in the room he sat in the floor by Kahlil's head. He was sprawled out across his queen-sized bed. "Shit sucks pops."

"Kahlil, watch your damn mouth."

"Dang Dad I don't get a pass?"

"No, you got to stop cussing." He scolded his son but the sad look on his face hurt Kahleno's feelings, so he decided to brighten his day a little. "You wanna know why you need to watch yo mouth?" Kahlil gave his father a skeptical look.

"Is this a trick question?" Kahleno shook his head at his son's old soul, he swear this kid had been there before.

"Sutton said we both got to watch our mouths, or she was gonna get the both of us." Kahlil's eyes widened and a smile spread across his face. "I knew that would get you smiling."

"She cut your hair." He said noticing that his dad had the same hair cut as he had. Kahleno nodded. "It ain't fresher than mine Dad but it's tight."

"You crazy, yo daddy fly."

"You been seeing my woman without me Dad? That ain't cool. I thought we were better than that."

"Yo, she ain't ya woman." Kahleno pointed at Kahlil who wore a scowl.

"Yes, the fu—Yes she is dad," he said catching himself.

"You see how she was looking at me?" he smiled from ear to ear showing all of his teeth.

"She was looking at you like that cause she gone be ya step mama."

"You a cock blocking busta dad." Kahleno burst out laughing again. "Can I call her?"

Kahleno looked at his son, he could tell that he wasn't feeling good. He was trying to stay in high spirits, but it was taking a lot out of him. So, anything to make him smile he was down to do. The fact that Kahlil wanted to speak to Sutton made him smile and further solidified what he already knew, she was the one for him. He just needed to get Trouble out of the way.

He didn't know if he was going about it the right way or not, but he didn't give a fuck. He was going to get her by any means necessary. If it meant forcing her bitch ass fiancé to hand her over than that's what the fuck it will take. He just hoped the shit didn't blow up in his face.

"Hello." The smooth sound of her voice flowed through the phone and he couldn't help the smile that spread across his face. "Hello."

"Hey beautiful." Sutton blushed from ear to ear. They had been talking on the phone for the last few days and she was starting to really feel him. Their conversation was so different from her's and Trouble's. Kahleno actually had something to say.

"Hey back."

"What's up baby?" Kahlil yelled from the back ground, his

voice was raspy, and he sounded like he wasn't himself and Sutton picked up on that right away.

"What's wrong with my guy?" she asked voice full of concern.

"See Dad, she said I was her gu—" he started but flew into a fit of coughing. Kahleno laid the phone down and lifted him up and began to pat him on the back. He reached for his power ranger cup to give him a drink.

"That's what you get for being fresh." Kahleno said and Kahlil laughed.

"Kahleno, is he okay." They could hear Sutton screaming from the phone. Kahleno picked it up and put it to his ear at the same time Karson had made it up the stairs and was in their presence.

"Sut?"

"Yeah I'm here is he okay? That sounded bad." She said was concerned that something was wrong with Kahlil, she had grown to like his little crazy self in the little time she's known his dad. She gotten the chance to see him twice and talked to him on the phone once and had fallen head over hills in love with him.

"Man, he good, he just wants your attention." Kahleno laughed and Kahlil reached down and grabbed the phone.

"Sutton I'm so sick, I need you to rub my back," Kahlil said making both Kahleno and Sutton laugh. "I need you Sutton."

"Kahleno can I talk to you for a minute?" Karson said from the door. Kahlil heard the anger in his mother's voice, he looked in her direction and knew that something made her mad. He just didn't know what.

"Let me see the phone son," Kahleno said knowing that Karson was about to be on her shit. He wasn't in the mood for it, so he prepared himself for the argument that was sure to come. "Hey beautiful, I'll call you later. I'm probably gone chill with Kahlil for the rest of the night, but I'll hit you tomorrow and maybe we can do lunch."

"Kahleno!" Karson yelled making sure that she was heard by whoever was on the phone. She thought it was extremely disrespectful for Kahleno to be on the phone with another woman, and the fact that this woman had been around her son was pissing her off even more.

She knew that she and Kahleno weren't together, but she thought he had more respect for her than to just throw the shit in her face knowing how she felt about him. Just hearing him call someone else beautiful hurt her and she was about to let him know about himself.

"Ahhh okay." The uncertainty in Sutton's voice pissed Kahleno off because he knew that she more than likely heard Karson. Her tone was rude, and Sutton more than likely felt it.

"No worries beautiful, Kahlil, tell Sutton good night." Kahleno glared at Karson daring her to say something. She shook her head on the brink of tears and stomped down the stairs.

"Night beautiful, I'll see you tomorrow." Kahlil started

making kissing noises in the phone and Sutton giggled at his silliness.

"Good night my handsome prince." She kissed in the phone and Kahlil smiled.

"Man lay yo ass down somewhere." Kahleno shook his head as he got up from the floor. "Aight, let me go down here and set some shit straight."

"I wasn't trying to start anything—"

"This ain't on you Sutton, we called you. You have nothing to apologize for so don't even try it. I'll call you when I get him sleep aight?"

"Okay." She didn't believe him. She had never dealt with a man with kids, but she'd heard the stories. The crazy baby mama stories and she didn't think she wanted to deal with that. Even though her and Kahleno was still getting to know each other and she still had to officially break things off with Trouble, things like that played a factor in how and if they would move forward.

"Don't do that but look I gotta go. I'll call you back." He hung up the phone and made his way down stairs.

When he got to the bottom of the stairs he watched as Karson pace like a mad woman across the living room floor. He shook his head and went to the kitchen and looked in the fridge to grab a beer, she kept a twelve pack in the fridge.

Popping the top, he took a swig and stood in the door way of the kitchen. When she realized that he had joined her she went on her rant.

"So, you seeing someone now?" she placed her hands on her hips.

"What I do and don't do ain't none of your concern Karson and you know that so why are you doing this to yourself?" Kahleno was trying his best to remain calm, he crossed his free hand across his chest and took a sip out of the beer. "What's this about?"

"Because you got bitches around my son!" she yelled louder than he was willing to deal with.

"Watch your fucking mouth!" he said through gritted teeth. "And lower your got damn tone. I'm still that nigga ain't shit changed." He warned her and she took a deep breath to calm her nerves, but it didn't work.

"Why do you have my son around other women?"

"I don't, I had *our* son around Sutton and that's because she cuts our hair."

"So, you trying to tell me you ain't fucking her?"

Kahleno took slow and deliberate steps towards her and when he got right up on her he stopped and looked down at her. Karson was bad, sexy as hell and she had a good head on her shoulders. His only problem with her was the fact that he couldn't trust her. She was sneaky and he didn't do well with that.

"No, I'm not fucking Sutton." She was holding her breath the whole time he spoke. "Not yet."

"You are so fucking disrespectful."

"No, you asked a got damn question and I answered it. How is that disrespectful?" He waited on her to answer him, but she didn't. Right now, she was trying to figure out how the two of them got to this point, she knew how but she never thought that it would go this far. "To be real, I'm feeling her, she's a damn good girl and she don't want shit from me. She didn't even know who I was. When I know for sure, I will bring her to introduce her to you. You do deserve to meet the woman that will be around your son outside of lining him up."

Karson felt like the wind had gotten knocked out of her. She grabbed her chest and forced herself not to cry. She couldn't believe the shit that was coming out of his mouth. He sounded like he had already made up his mind that she was it, so where does that leave her?

"You don't even know this bitch."

"Listen, I'm trying to be patient with yo dumb ass because of the situation but you keep trying me. Don't call her out of her name. She wouldn't even disrespect you like that so show her the same damn respect and that's the last time I'm saying the shit."

"Wow, it's like that Kahleno. After everything that we've been through. After all that I've been to you? It's like that?"

"You acting like I'm the one that fucked this up," his voice raised just a few octaves. "You did this shit, you fucked this family up."

"And I said I was sorry."

"Sorry don't fix everything Karson, I forgave you because if I hadn't, you'd be floating in somebody's fucking river and you know that. The fact that you standing here on that good bullshit lets you know that shits good. I just don't want to be with you and it ain't shit you can do to change that."

"What if I brought a man around our son?"

"Then that's on you, as long as that nigga do right by my shorty, and I get to meet him then that's what's up. A nigga will be happy to finally get you off his shit."

Karson felt her heart shatter, her chest got tight, and everything he said after that was gibberish. She felt like she was having an out-of-body experience and she didn't know how to handle what she was feeling.

It was over, any chance that she thought she had to get her family back was gone and it hurt. There was no other way to explain it. When she looked up into his eyes, they were emotionless. Karson was trying to think back to when he could have got with someone and flipped on her that quick.

Karson cleared her throat and wiped her eyes. "Are you staying here? Or are you ahhh umm or ahhh are you leaving?" She looked everywhere in the room besides at Kahleno.

"I don't know, my son asked me to but I'm not if it's going to be an issue."

"I would never create an issue for you when it comes to Kahlil, Kahleno and you know that." pain dripped from every word she spoke and it made Kahleno feel like shit but there was nothing that he could do about it, he would never be what she needed him to be.

Karson turned and headed in the kitchen and Kahleno made his way back upstairs to check on Kahlil. When he got in the room, he was surprised to fine Kahlil sleep. Karson peeked in the room and tossed him a blanket and a pillow.

Kahleno had himself comfortable on the floor of the room and turned the TV on the NFL network. Football Preseason had started, and his Steelers were playing the Panthers. Scrolling through his social media he came across a post that Sutton had posted. It read...

"Sometimes we fight so hard to keep those doors open that common sense should have slammed long ago. Don't miss out on your future trying to play catch up with the past... especially if your future is as bright as mine." (smiling and heart emoji's)

Kahleno screenshot the message and texted it to asking her if the post had anything to do with him. He laid down on the floor waiting for a response. A few minute had passed and Kahleno looked down at his phone and still nothing. He was about to call her when he heard soft wails coming from Karson's room.

He knew that he should have just minded his business, but he did feel bad about how that shit went down. It wasn't that he hated her, in fact he still had love for her as the mother of his son. Getting up and making his way to the hallway and in front of her bedroom door.

Slowly opening the door, he walked in and saw her laying on the floor with a picture of him and her, he was holding Kahlil in one arm and her in the other. He smiled down at the picture because at one point they were happy.

"Karson," he said softly making her jump. She slid the picture under the bed and wiped her eyes with the back of her hand. Sitting up, positioning herself against the bed she looked at him and shook her head.

"Please get out," she said as more tears fell down her face. Kahleno got down on the floor with her and pulled her into his lap. Getting that close to her could possibly cross some lines that he's worked so hard to draw. She needed this right now and with all that they had been through it was the least he could do.

"Come here man, look stop crying." Kahleno wiped her eyes and then pulled her into him. "You better than this Karson, when I met you, you didn't need a man for shit."

"I still don't."

"Okay so what is all of this for? You know what it is, shit happened, and you know what I say..."

"Everything happens for a reason." She finished his sentence and then buried her head in his chest. "I know that but it's just hard just thinking about you doing all of the things with another woman that you did to and for me. I still love you and I can't help that. I'm trying to let it go but it's hard, you were my everything."

"Look at it like this, if we were meant to be shit wouldn't have fell apart so easily. I wouldn't have walked away so easy and you wouldn't have felt the need to steal a nigga's sperm to make sure you had a spot in a nigga's life."

"That's not why—"

"That's bullshit and you know it Karson, you did that because you thought having multiple kids by me would keep me and that's not true. I'm an amazing father and everyone knows that so I would have took care of my kids but that didn't guarantee you my last name. And you out of all people should've known that." he kissed her cheek and she looked him in the eyes.

She hadn't been this close to him in so long and she had to admit that it felt good. His eyes told her that the words that were coming out of his mouth was what he really meant but she was holding on to the chance that maybe, just maybe if she took things to another level. He would see that with her is where he wanted to be.

Karson wasn't a desperate female by far, but she knew what she wanted, and she wanted Kahleno. She wanted her family and she felt like she deserved it. Her mom and dad raised her and her siblings as a tight knit family and she wanted the same thing for her kids.

Throwing caution to the wind, she crashed her lips against his, she closed her eyes and kissed him with all her might. When she realized that he hadn't kissed her back she opened her eyes and met his.

"The fuck you doing Karson, this shit ain't gone make a difference one way or another. We can fuck right now, and I'll leave here still feeling the same way. Sex don't move me ma and you know it." he looked at her and he could see the hope in her eyes. He should have just got up and left but he didn't.

"I know that Kahleno, I need this right now." She kissed his lips again and still no reciprocation.

Sighing heavily, he closed his eyes and threw his head back. He was single and could do what the fuck he wanted to do but for some reason this didn't feel right. Sutton popped in his head and he knew that he was feeling her something serious, but she was still with that nigga Trouble. Kahleno had been chasing her and hadn't had pussy in weeks but he knew that if he slid in Karson, it would be starting a whole bunch of shit.

"Nah we can't do this I don't want to confuse things." Kahleno said with his head still thrown back. Karson climbed off of his lap and he got prepared for the argument that was sure to come but was met with the head of his dick touching the back of her throat. "Fuck!"

She slowly sucked and bobbed up and down on his shaft, while her small hands found his balls and played with them. She knew that head was Kahleno's weakness. He had expressed on more than one occasion that the feel of a woman's warm thick tongue on his dick did something to him, so Karson made sure to use her tongue to the best of her abilities.

"Shit Karson, just like that. Fuck!" He knew he should have stopped her, but he couldn't. Karson always did know what to do when it came to pleasing him. That's how she almost got him caught up. "Shit go faster and suck harder, yeah just like that."

Karson bobbed up and down on his shaft like her life depended on it and in a way it did. She needed him to remember but what she didn't know is that his attention was somewhere else. Sutton plagued his thoughts right as his nut hit the pit of his stomach.

"I'm about to nut," he called out right before he filled her mouth up with the seeds she so desperately wanted. Not wanting to scare him off she swallowed every last drop and smiled up at him. "Fuck girl."

"You have to at least miss that." He hated that she sounded so insecure in who she was. The Karson that he met all those years ago wasn't this woman in front of him. He grabbed her face and brought her forehead to his. She moved closer and straddled him.

"You're better than this Karson, and you know it."

"But I want this," she raised up and slid down on his dick that was still hard from her giving him that *remember me* head. "Can I have this, if only for tonight."

"Fuck Karson," Kahleno looked down and watched as she rolled her body into him real nice and slow. Her tight walls were wrapped around his dick so tight, that on top of how wet she was had him about to bust prematurely. Just as the thought went through his mind so did the fact that he didn't have on a rubber. "Watch out Karson, I need to wrap up." He grabbed her waist and she started moving faster.

"No, it's okay, it's okay." She moved faster and he could feel that shit in the pit of his gut.

"Move, Karson." He gave her once last chance to move and when she didn't, he got pissed and tossed her off of him, causing her to hit her head on the dresser.

"Owwww. Fuck!" she yelled as she leaned up and grabbed her head.

"What the fuck you think you doing, huh? What you was gone try and pull a nut out of a nigga? You a dumb bitch!"

"Oh, it's okay for you to disrespect me, the mother of your child but get all puffed out when I talk about your bitch."

"Fuck yeah especially when you acting like a stupid bitch." He jumped in her face. "How fucking desperate are you?"

Kahleno didn't know what the fuck was wrong with Karson, she was acting dumb as hell for the last few weeks and he hated it. He tried his best to stay away but he couldn't do that because of Kahlil, and he loved his son, making sure to see him at least three times a week.

"Just get out."

"Yeah, I need to do that before I beat your got damn ass." Kahleno fixed the ball shorts he had on and went to his son's room to get dressed. He prayed that his son was still sleep because he didn't want to have to explain to him that his mother was being a bitch.

After he was dressed and gathered his things, he kissed his son and walked down the stairs. He could hear Karson in the kitchen, and he wasn't for her shit, so he headed for the door.

"I don't want my son around her."

"Fuck you and that bullshit you talking! Tell my son I'll be here tomorrow!"

"No, you won't, we gone get a schedule and you'll stick to it. I'm moving on with my life like you moving on with yours. And I can't do that if you popping up anytime you want to."

Kahleno took a deep breath before he snapped her neck. Taking slow and deliberate steps towards her, caused Karson to freeze where she was. She knew what kind of man Kahleno was and how he could be, but she was pissed he denied her and that he was trying to move on with his life, without her.

"I will see my son when the fuck I want to see my son and I dare you or anybody else to try and fucking stop me." he released an evil chuckle. "To think all of this is because a nigga don't want you no more because of some shady shit that you did!" he pointed at her and she jumped. "I'm not the person to have as an enemy and you of all people should know that. Don't make shit hard for you, it ain't worth it ma."

With that he turned and walked out of the apartment and left a very hurt Karson to wallow in her own pity. Kahleno knew that shit with Karson was about to get sticky and he had himself to blame for it.

CHAPTER ELEVEN

Joker's Wild

"Aye turn the music up!" Menz yelled to the DJ who was spinning his favorite 21 Savage song. That shit was hitting hard and the X pill that he had took was taking him on a ride. Menz was supposed to be helping his workers to set up a new house on the west side because the other one got too hot.

After everything was set up Menzell got the urge to throw a party and have some fun. All the work was done, and the house wasn't due to open until the next day. He didn't see any harm in having a few people over, getting a DJ and ordering a few pizzas.

Yeah it was drugs in the house and money, but no one here was dumb enough to steal from his family. Not and live to tell about it. He was in the mood to get fucked up and fuck a couple bitches tonight.

"My nigga." Trouble said pushing through the crowd. He looked around, he wasn't into the drug game like that, he knew he wasn't built for it but even he knew that you weren't supposed to throw a party at a trap house. That was the quickest way to get the police called.

"Awww shit Trouble in the house!" Menz yelled over the music and everyone turned in their direction. Trouble nodded and then headed in the direction of the makeshift bar. He was nervous and it showed in his behavior, Menz picked up on it too. "The fuck wrong with you nigga? You the police or something, you all nervous and shit. You wearing a wire or some shit?" Menz asked now grilling Trouble.

"Nigga fuck you! If anybody should be worrying about someone being shady it's you. Why in the fuck would you call me here knowing what was up with me and your peoples? And then you throwing fucking parties in a trap house, nigga you trying to get yo ass beat."

"Man fuck them! They don't run shit I do! They sit back and collect money like little bitches. I do all the work. They don't do shit." Menz puffed out his chest, his father had been getting in his head about how the *family business* was being ran. Even though they weren't blood they were still considered family.

Menz's father married Mega's sister Meka when Menzell was a young boy. His mother never wanted him. She left when

Menz was first born because she figured out who her baby's father really was, a nobody.

Menzell Senior, or Senior as everyone likes to call him was a lot like his son. He wanted life handed to him. He didn't really want to work for anything. He saw opportunities and jumped at them. Then when he worked his way in, he pretended to work much more than he was.

Senior worked alongside Mega, well actually he was Mega's runner. Just like his son. He hated it, he felt like Mega should have had him in the forefront not doing his dirty work. He was never man enough to say anything about it, so now he was living through his son. Filling his head with all kinds of things to try and get him to get to the top, something he never did.

"Yeah I hear all that rah rah bullshit but them niggas don't play when it comes to their money and everyone knows that. Even you, you geeked right now so I'ma let you have that but I'm out. I ain't got time to be getting caught up with yo peoples. I gotta find a way to get this money."

"Nigga you worried about that," Menz shook his head. "If that nigga wanted you dead you would not be walking the streets right now. He wants yo girl and the way you be dogging her ass out, you don't give that much of a fuck about her." Menz was starting to slur, his high was kicking in.

"Easy for you to say, it ain't yo bitch."

"If my cousin get his hands on her, she won't be yours either." Menz laughed and spotted April across the room. He rolled his eyes in the back of his head and got ready for the bullshit. "If she nag anything like her, just let him have her G."

"Why don't you just let me hold the money?" Menz wanted to laugh, if anyone knew him Trouble did so he should have known that there was no way in hell that he would be letting him hold a got damn thing.

"I ain't really got it, I took that big hit the other week and my bitch ass cousins making me pay that shit back with interest," Menz said partially telling the truth, Kahleno was making him pay back the money he lost with that last shipment but Menz had more money than he knew what to do with. Even though he was at the bottom of the totem when it came to family, they still laced him well.

"Damn, I gotta go figure some shit out." Trouble turned and was about to leave until he came face to face with the round face beauty. His tongue swept across his bottom lip and a smirk spread across his face. "I'm Trouble."

"Yes, you are," Lexus said cheesing from ear to ear. She knew that if he was hanging with Menz then he had money and was someway connected to the Maler empire. She didn't know who he was, but she just wanted a piece of that pie and she planned to get just that.

Trouble grabbed her by the hand and led her back to the makeshift bar and grabbed her a drink. Menz walked over and laid a variety of X pills on the bar and Lexus snatched up two, she ate one and tucked the other one in her pocketbook. Trouble smiled at her. He knew that she liked to have fun and he was all for it.

"Sutton who?" Menz said in Trouble's ear and he smiled

but in the back of his mind he knew that if it came down to choosing between Sutton and another woman it would always be Sutton. That's just how it was, and it wasn't going to change.

Lexus and Trouble sat at the bar and got to know each other, while everyone else around them had the time of their lives. It didn't take long for him to get her to take him home, she had ate a X pill and she was horny. She called Kahleno a few times and he cleared her every time.

Trouble was sexy and from what she felt his dick was big, she knew that she would at least have a good time.

"April, you good? Me and Trouble about to slip out." Lexus smiled at her sister. Her sister looked Trouble up and down, she knew that she had seen him somewhere, but she couldn't put her finger on where she had seen him. Maybe it was from him knowing Menz she didn't know but he had sneaky eyes and she didn't trust him.

"You don't know this nigga."

"You didn't know that nigga either but look at you." She pointed to April's stomach and April smiled. She was pregnant because she wanted to be, there was no oops about it. Nodding her head, she high fived her sister.

Trouble looked back and forth between the sisters and was almost second guessing taking that ride with her. Pussy was pussy though and if he was lucky just maybe he could squeeze a few dollars out of her.

"WHAT THE FUCK?" the voice boomed from the front

of the house all the way to the back of the house where the makeshift bar was.

Menzell's whole body language changed, where he once was tough and bold, he now cowered under the sound of a Maler. Trouble stood by as he watched the youngest brother, AD walk over to the DJ booth and knock all of his equipment over and then proceeded to turn on all the lights.

Spiff looked around and he couldn't believe what the fuck was going on, he gave Menzell one job, one fucking job and he couldn't even do that shit right. He searched the room for Menzell, and he had gone to the back of the kitchen to do something.

"Where the fuck is Menzell bitch ass.?" Spiff's voice boomed just as loud as AD.

AD was so mad he could have spit fire. He was gripping the handle of his gun so fucking tight that he could feel his finger tips about to burn. Adoreé couldn't stand Menz and he had good reason, when he was younger and got in all that trouble, he was defending him. He never told his daddy that shit but that's why. Menz went out there and started all that shit only for AD to clean it up and when the shit hit the fan Menz disappeared and left him hanging, hadn't fucked with him since.

"Ayyeee what's up family?" Menz's voice slightly trembled. If it was Cassidy or Kahleno he wouldn't have been as scared to deal with this situation but Adoreé was the crazier of the three and he was unpredictable.

"What the fuck is this?" Spiff said.

"Oh, we handled all the shit we needed to handle for tonight, so we decided to have a little get together," Menz said looking around. April stepped up and put her arm on his shoulder and AD grilled her.

"Who the fuck is we?" AD's voice boomed through the room and everyone looked around, there was no way that any one of them would openly say that they had anything to do with any of this. "So, what y'all saying is ain't nobody have shit to do with this dumb shit?" Again no one said anything. Adoreé nodded his head.

Without saying another word, he walked over and popped Menz in the mouth. He hit him again and again, begging him to fight back so he would have a reason to kill him. Adoreé knew that he wouldn't fight back because he was bitch made just like his daddy.

No one tried to stop him, no one said anything, they knew better. If it was anyone else, they would be in a ditch with a bullet in their brain, but the Maler Brothers loved their Aunt Meka so for now he just took the ass whooping.

"Bro that's enough," Spiff said tone lacking authority. He wasn't scared of shit and half the time he welcomed death, but AD was his boy and he wasn't trying to go there with him.

"Stop you're going to kill him." April jumped on AD's back and that pissed him off further. He reached around and pulled her down on the ground and pulled his gun out and stuck it in her mouth.

"You ever put your nasty ass on me again and I swear I'll

blow your got damn brains out and send them to your hoe ass mama. Are we clear?"

"Please don't hurt my sister AD please!" Lexus said face full of tears, she turned to look for the fine nigga who she had planned to take home, but he was nowhere to be found. She was pissed, he now had no chance in hell with her. He was scary and she knew it.

Trouble had left long ago, after AD delivered the first blow, he knew that was his time to go. That wasn't his fight and if the shoe was on the other foot, Menz wouldn't hesitate to bounce on him.

"Shut the fuck up bitch before I light yo hoe ass up," Spiff growled at Lexus who immediately shut her mouth. She didn't know what the fuck was going on, but she knew that her sister could deal with these crazy ass people, but she was done after tonight.

"Are we clear bitch?" AD asked again, this time through clenched teeth. She nodded her head as fresh tears fell down her face. AD got up and looked down at her with a grimace on his face. Menz was moaning in pain but AD had no sympathy. "I want this shit cleaned up in an hour, all my shit better be accounted for and I want all these muthafucking people out of here. ONE FUCKING HOUR! Or somebody ain't gone be breathing."

"And all y'all muthafuckas that's supposed to be working and let his dumb ass talk y'all into this. I'ma holla at y'all tomorrow," Spiff said and all the workers that were in attendance swallowed hard, they knew what that meant. They were about to be out of a fucking job.

Spiff and AD made their way out of the house and back to the strip club where they were before they got the call. The little nigga Vinny put them up on game, not on no snitch shit but letting them know the block was hot. He had been putting in work, so he would be taking Menz's place here more than likely.

CHAPTER TWELVE

Last Resort

"Trouble if you don't bring me my money back, I swear I'm gonna get my brother to come after you and you know how that go. Don't think he won't blast yo ass now bring me my money. You know I got kids and I needed to get their school stuff. I'm not playing with you Trouble. If I don't hear from you soon, not only will you be running for your life, I'll tell your precious Sutton that you and I been fucking, and you got me pregnant. Now fuck with me."

Trouble pressed end on his phone after listening to the message that Sunny had left. She sounded like she was pissed, and he had plans on stopping by her place, dicking her down and giving her back her money but things hadn't worked out in his favor the last few days.

He had found out that Sutton changed the locks on him

that fast. On top of the fact that he had been winning all week at the casino and Kahleno even gave him an extra week to come up with the twenty g's. Something about his son being sick and him feeling generous, either way Trouble was grateful.

"What the fuck did I do!" Trouble yelled at himself in the mirror. He was currently at Cami's house and they were kicking it. She was a cool ass female, she was just too hood for him. He wanted someone that was green to the streets.

Sutton's dad was the man back in the day, but he shielded her away from that life. She was clueless to anything street wise and that worked to Trouble's advantage. He wasn't as street as everyone thought he was, but he was able to get by.

"Baby what's wrong?" Cami asked walking in the room with a Joe Boxer panty and sports bra set on. It was sexy on her, but he wished she would wear shit like Sutton, Victoria Secret, stuff like Sutton would wear. "Here hit this blunt."

Trouble looked back at her and shook his head. He grabbed the blunt and threw himself on the couch. Everything was falling apart for him right now and he didn't know how to come up out of this slump.

"Man, I'm in some shit." He tried his hand at Cami.

"What's up baby, you know I got you." He passed the blunt back to her and watched as he put it to her lips and inhaled like a champ. Trouble thought that was so un-lady like but chose not to comment on it.

"I got into some shit with the Maler boys," he glanced at her and she lowered the blunt. Cami knew what that meant, and she honestly didn't want any parts of it. Spiff was her brother and one of their top lieutenants so if she got in some shit with them, she would never hear the end of it. "I owe them like twenty bands."

"Dammmnnnn, how the fuck you get away with that?" she knew the Maler brothers, hell she worked for them and she knew that they never let anyone get that far in debt.

"Menz is my nigga and he been vouching for a nigga."

Cami started to laugh, Trouble didn't see this as a laughing matter. "Man, that nigga ain't got no pull, I got more pull than he do. Shit, they hate his ass so if anything, that's gone make them come at you more. There's got to be another reason." She hit the blunt again.

"Nah that's it, but I need to borrow some money." Again, she laughed, she had never been with a man that needed money from her. She normally dated the niggas she worked with but when she met Trouble, he sweet talked her right out of her draws. Cami was a pretty girl. Dark skinned, she wore weave down to her ass, she was a little on the slim side, but she had enough to keep you interested. "What the fuck is so funny?"

"Oh wait, you serious?" Cami asked and he nodded his head. She folded her arms across her chest pushing up her perky C cups. She was feeling Trouble and that was no doubt, but she didn't know if she was feeling him enough to just come up off twenty thousand dollars. "Look we cool and all, but I can't just give you all that money not knowing if I'ma get it back or not. I would be dumb as hell to do that."

"But I thought we were cool."

"Yeah we are cool but we ain't in no relationship. You ain't my nigga, hell if you was my nigga you damn sure wouldn't be needing to borrow money from me. Nah I can't do that."

"Come on, I'll give it right back."

"How can you say for sure? If that was the case, you wouldn't need the money now." She raised a brow and Trouble jumped up.

"Fuck you then."

"Cool my nigga, keep that same energy." She said not really giving a fuck. She liked Trouble and his dick game was A1, but she wasn't that pressed, not to sit there and be disrespected. She shook her head and pointed for him to leave. "You can leave playboy."

Trouble didn't say anything else, he knew he would have to let her cool down because right now he didn't have anywhere else to stay. Sunny wasn't fucking with him right now and Sutton changed the locks on him, Cami was his only option.

"Look my bad a nigga in a bad place."

"That ain't my issue."

"I know babe, my bad. I'll hit you up later." His attempt at reconciliation was a fail, she pointed at the door for him to leave, which he did. Cami wasn't trying to get caught up in his shit, and no matter how good the sex was, she knew that she may have to let him go.

~

Sutton stared at the mirror as she examined herself in it. Her long hair brushed past her bra strap, her perky breast sat up nice in the new bra she had just bought. Her smooth golden skin was blemish free and her light eyes only added to her sexiness.

Mentally preparing herself for this meeting with Trouble was bothering her to the point that she thought about cancelling and just breaking up with him over a text message. She knew that would be wrong and she had to get the closure that both of them would need.

Opting to wear an off the shoulder, pale pink flowy shirt with a cute pair of khaki shorts that barely covered her ass and exposed her thick thighs. She paired her ensemble with a nice pair of pink strappy sandals that she got on sale at Forever 21.

Once she was dressed, she headed downstairs and straight to the fridge to get a drink because she was sure she was going to need it. The ringing of her phone jarred her from her task, she looked at it and realized it was her girl.

“Well hello hoe, ain’t heard from you in a while. Mr. Saque been had all of your attention.” Sutton commented on the fact that she hadn’t seen or talked to her best friend in so long and she kinda felt some kind of way. She felt like when it came to men she was always put on the back burner, unless she needed her to come with her to check up on them.

“My bad boo, you know I love you and I just seen you at work so don’t even act like that.” She giggled into the phone.

"Ummhmmm for like two seconds. Enough to say hey and bye that's it. Then you rushed to the back so you can call Saque."

"Awww boo, you feel neglected. Well let's plan a girl's day, I'll let Saque know ahead of time." Piper said looking back at Saque who was staring dead at her. She knew that if it came down to it and she had plans with Sutton and Saque wanted her time, the choice was simple for her. She knew it made her a shitty friend, but she also knew that Sutton would always be there.

"Yeah, yeah I hear ya. I don't exist to you when you gotta nigga. I should be used to it by now."

"Sttoooppp it Sut! I don't do that to you when you trying to figure stuff out with Trouble."

"That's because whether I'm with someone or not I don't neglect my friends, girl. The difference between me and you is when a man comes into my life, he doesn't make me, he makes me better. Get it?"

"Ugh well let me let you go because you seem to be in a mood and you taking it out on me." Sutton laughed because Piper could be so selfish at times and she hated it, but she loved her friend dearly.

"Okay Pipe, I love you and be careful." With that Sutton hung up the phone and took a shot followed by another one.

Shaking her head, she had to stop thinking that everyone was like her because that wasn't the truth. She was built different and she took pride in that, her dad taught her at an early age to never let a man define her which is why he was so mad that she was allowing herself to go through the shit with Trouble.

Sutton didn't feel like Trouble's problems changed who she was because at the end of the day she didn't need him anymore than she needed the light coat of makeup that she decided to add to her look tonight. That's what made her different. She did things because she wanted to, not because she felt like she had to.

Grabbing her keys and clutch, she made sure all of her lights were turned off and she left out to head to the restaurant. Trouble had begged her to allow him to pick her up, but she refused. She knew that after she told him that she didn't want to see him anymore that he would more than likely flip out.

What was normally a fifteen-minute ride to TGIFriday's at Northlake mall, turned into a thirty-minute drive because Sutton was stalling. Trouble had texted her twenty minutes ago saying that he was there waiting at the bar. She needed to get this over with but then again, she really didn't want to hurt him but too much had happened.

"I'm meeting someone." Sutton told the hostess the minute she entered the building. "Ah there he is." She pointed at Trouble and the hostess gave her a nasty look and rolled her eyes. Sutton was two seconds from getting in her ass but decided against it. She didn't have time for the petty bullshit, she had bigger fish to fry. "Damn are you fucking her?" Sutton asked when Trouble was in her space.

"What? What are you talking about baby, why in the hell

would I invite you here if that was the case?" Trouble glanced in the direction of the hostess station and watched as CeeCee texted away on her phone. He was sure that she was calling her sister, Sunny to tell her that he was here with Sutton.

"You sure because the little beads of sweat forming on ya eyebrows is telling me something different playboy. Let me find out."

Sutton was slowly getting pissed at the situation. Yes, she was there to break up with him, but she couldn't sit and say that the thought of him cheating on her while they were together wouldn't make her mad. She glared at the hostess who was looking their way.

"Baby fuck all that, that hoe tried to holla at me when I walked in here and I played that hoe to the left. I told her that she couldn't hold a candle to my girl, and she didn't take that shit too well." A nervous chuckle left his lips causing Sutton to shake her head.

"Look, I can't even sit here and say that I believe anything that's coming out of your mouth right now. What the fuck man?" Sutton chewed on her bottom lip trying not to go off because at this point it was irrelevant. Trouble could see the disappointment in her eyes, he saw something else too but there's no way that he would accept it.

"Baby I love you, I want you to know that. I've done some dumb shit and I don't deserve a second chance to be with you. The day I put that ring on your finger," he started and looked down and then swallowed his words.

"Oh, what ring, the one you promised me a long time ago

that I never got?" Sutton laughed. When he asked her to marry him, he was high off of a winning streak and promised to go out and buy her a big ass diamond. Well, needless to say, tomorrow never came because the next day he gambled away all of his winnings.

"Baby fuck all of that, I just want to start over fresh." This conversation was not going the way that Trouble had hoped it would. He needed her on his side, he needed her to be there for him. Especially if it came down to him having to ask her to do the unthinkable. Which right now, seemed like the last resort. His hope was to see how this conversation went, get her in bed and sex her into agreeing. He didn't know if that would work but he was hoping for his sake.

"Trouble, listen. At this point I just don't see anything good coming out of this." Sutton pointed back and forth between the two of them. "You're too deep in and I'm not trying to get caught up in your bullshit."

"Who told you that shit, Kahleno?" Trouble threw himself back in the seat and glared at her. Since that day at the salon, when he caught him in there, Trouble felt like Sutton had been acting crazy and he wasn't feeling it. He felt like Kahleno was the reason he was in this position with Sutton in the first place. Everything was fine until he popped up at her shop. "You fucking him Sutton? Ever since I saw y'all together you been on that bullshit. Locking me out of the house that I help pay for—"

"Since fucking when?" Sutton sat up in the seat ready to tear him a new one. Now here she come ready to be civil and make this split easier for the both of them, but Trouble was starting to piss her off. "First off I ain't got to fuck a nigga to have him ready to pay my bills and you of all people should know that. I'm not you Trouble, I didn't throw this relationship away for my own selfish reasons you did!" she yelled louder than she intended, drawing stares from those closest to them. "Sorry," Sutton apologized relaxing back in her seat.

Sutton didn't feel that Trouble loved her enough to manage his gambling and the fact that it was affecting her livelihood didn't sit well with her. The gambling debt was no longer balancing out and he didn't see that, and she wasn't inclined to be explaining to a grown man what he was doing wrong. Now, it was someone else's fault his world was falling apart, typical Trouble.

"I can't believe you Sutton, I never took you as the type." Trouble released an angry chuckle.

"What type is that?" Sutton moved back to the edge of her seat.

"The gold-digging hoe type." It was Sutton's turn to chuckle, pinching the bridge of her nose in an attempt to calm down as she shook her head at his ignorance.

"If that was the case, what the fuck was I doing with your broke ass all this time?" She tilted her head to the side and Trouble's nose flared. This conversation had taken a turn for the worse and he didn't know how to recover from it or if he wanted to. He was pissed at the thought that Kahleno had already been with Sutton.

"You think that man want you? You think he give a fuck

about you?" Trouble said leaning in to meet her stare. A sneaky smirk appeared on his face and Sutton glared at him. The shit was pissing her off to the point she wanted to reach over the table and slap the shit out of him.

"You know what, I'm done with this. I came here to be civilized and to tell you that I don't want to be with your anymore. Send me an address and I will have your shit shipped there. I didn't want any bad blood with us because when it comes down to it, I do love you, but I don't feel like that shit is reciprocated. The only thing you care about is yourself and the fucking crap tables. I deserve better than this and I deserve better than you." She stood up and pointed at him.

They now had every eye in the establishment on them, but she no longer cared. She was over Troubles shit. She didn't know if it was the fact that Trouble was saying that Kahleno was possibly playing her or if she was just that over him and his shit, or both. Sutton just knew that she was beyond pissed. The best option for her was to remove herself from the situation.

"Oh, you deserve Kahleno who still fucking with his baby's mother, Lexus hoe ass and God knows who else." He matched her tone. "That same Kahleno that offered to clear my debt just to have a weekend with yo hoe ass." He seethed. Sutton's eyes stretched and she knew that her cheeks were red, she could feel her face get hot. "Yeah, that's how much he thinks about you, you are only worth a measly twenty bands." Trouble grabbed his stomach and laughed. He knew he had just won but Sutton had something for him.

"But you agreed to it, though right? That's why you invited me here?" she glared down at him and he immediately stopped laughing and realized what he had just done, he had just fucked himself. "Yeah, tell me what kind of man even thinks to let another man get away with his fiancée? What you think we was gone watch cartoons all weekend? Nah he's told me what he wanted to do to me so I'm sure that weekend would have nailed the coffin that much tighter on this bullshit relationship."

"Sut I—"

"Nah bro, keep that same fucking energy. If I wasn't done with you then you best believe I am now and just so you know..." she leaned in and whispered to him. "He just dropped twenty measly bands off at the shop to pay my mortgage." With that she laughed and stood up.

Trouble was so pissed that he could literally see himself hitting her in the mouth repeatedly, he wasn't stupid though. He knew who Hudson was and there was no mistake in what he would do to him if he hit his precious Sutton.

"TROUBLE!" hearing his name across the restaurant made him cringe. He knew that CeeCee was calling her sister and he was kicking himself for not leaving when he saw her. The argument that ensued between him and Sutton made him forget the drama that was brewing.

He tried telling the bitch that he was working on getting her money back, but she didn't care about that. In CeeCee's eyes, Trouble was a bum that her sister was in love with because she knew he belonged to Sutton. She needed to see that nigga for who he was and leave him the fuck alone.

"You can leave, I'm sure that nigga looking for you." Trouble's words were dripping with hate, but Sutton could see the worry in his eyes, his shit was about to come to the forefront, and she was gonna be front and center.

"Nah I'm trying to figure out why Sunny here and calling your name like that." Sutton's hands went on her hips and she turned towards Sunny who had a smirk on her face.

"Go the hell on somewhere Sunny," Trouble said trying to get up.

"No Trouble, where is my got damn money? That money was for my kids!" she yelled at him. "Why in the hell would you steal from me?"

"Why in the hell wouldn't he steal from you, dumb ass?" Sutton said feeling her temperature rise, she knew good and damn well that he wasn't sleeping with Sunny. She didn't know exactly how she would handle this if he was. "So, you fucking her too?"

"Yes!" Sunny answered before Trouble could and he was pissed. He ran his hands down his face and then looked at Sutton with guilt in his eyes.

"Are you fucking kidding me?" Sutton said more to herself than anyone else. "Nah this has got to be a fucking joke."

Sutton ran her tongue across her lip and looked down at the ground. *10...9...8...7...6...5... fuck this.* She thought to herself before she growled and tried to rush Sunny. Trouble grabbed her up in the air and pulled her back so that she was far enough away.

Sunny wasn't stupid enough to try and sneak her because she knew that Sutton could fight, she'd seen her in action a time or two when they were younger. Sunny didn't have the hands god gave her so she resorted to running her mouth.

"Don't get mad at me because you wasn't handling yo business at home and he came to me. I wasn't trying to go there with him he came on to me," she lied, and Sutton laughed. She always laughed when she was mad.

"You a muthafuckin lie Sunny and you know it. You followed me out of the salon one day and I fucked you in my car. I never came on to you, you always called me so don't do that shit."

"And that makes it better?" Sutton struggled against his hold until he let her go and she hauled back and slapped the piss out of him. "Don't you ever put your hands on me again. You sorry muthafucka. Is that where you disappear to when you ain't home huh?" Sutton was making a scene and she was pissed at herself for it, but she felt like she deserved answers.

"Well his time is split between me and Cami," Sunny said matter-of-factly.

"You a dumb bitch, you just fucked yourself for a nigga that stole from you. A nigga that took money from your kids, idiot. A nigga that didn't give enough fucks about you to fuck you in his car and a public street and you proud of that?" Sutton's words cut through Sunny's whole tough girl exterior like a knife. She made her feel so damn small but

Sunny never dropped her head even though her eyes told it all.

"Sutton—"

"SAVE IT!" Tears were threatening to fall but she refused to let them. She was pissed beyond words. "You bitch, are fired. You have until Monday to come get your shit or it will be on the side of the road. And you, a moving crew will be at my house on Monday morning, you can either meet them there or tell me where to drop your shit."

"Baby—"

"NO! I don't have time for this shit. Got me out here looking stupid fucking with bitches that are beneath me. I'm so mad at myself for even letting y'all get me out of character, I got too much to lose to entertain this bullshit." Sutton walked back over to the table and grabbed her clutch and keys. "Y'all deserve each other and I hope he makes your life miserable. Don't forget.... Monday." And with that Sutton was gone.

Sunny released the tears that she had been holding in for so long. She didn't know what she was going to do now, her ego got the best of her. Taking something that belonged to Sutton was a dream of hers she just didn't know that it would cause her the one thing that she was proud of, her job.

Chamber of Beauty had helped to build her clientele so much that she sometimes had to turn people around and now she was back at square one. She looked into the eyes of Trouble who was staring at her with hate in his eyes.

She turned to walk away, and he grabbed her arm, "I guess

I'm yours now." He smirked and she looked at him and shook her head. Jerking away she glared at him.

"Fuck you, I want my money or else I'm calling my brother and you don't want that." She pointed at him. He was about to jack her up before her sister CeeCee walked up with a knife in her hand.

"I wish the fuck you would."

Trouble shook his head and turned to walk out of the restaurant. This day went from shit to even more shit in a matter of minutes. Fuck!

CHAPTER THIRTEEN

Changes

Mega looked at all of his sons sitting in the family farm house, he was blessed to have each and every one of them. All he ever wanted was a family full of boys to carry on the family name and that's what God and his wife blessed him with. He had been very fortunate in his 44 years of living.

"What you over there thinking about Pops?" Cassidy leaned back in the recliner as he took a bite of an orange with the peel still on it.

"Life son, just life."

"Yo pops you been acting weird as fuck since you got here, anything we should know about?" Kahleno the more observant of the three pointed out. His dad's vibe was off, and he could sense that something was wrong he just hoped it wasn't anything to do with his mother. "Is it moms? Is she sick? Is that why she didn't come with you?" Kahleno fired off question after question.

Mega smiled at his son, out of all three of his boys, Kahleno reminded him so much of himself. From the way he liked to take control of every situation, how he handled business, to the way he just tried to assess a situation that he had no idea about. Shaking his head, Mega thought about the secret that he was holding and knew that it would hurt Kahleno the most.

"Nah, me and ya mama hit a rough patch. She thought we needed some space, so I flew here to be with my boys. I talked to her last night though and she'll be here soon, and she wants y'all to cook for her."

"Nah pops don't even try it, she wants you to cook for her and you trying to throw that shit off on us," AD said pointing to his dad and they all fell out laughing. AD knew that his mom loved his dad's cooking and when he made her mad that was the only way to make up for it.

"Whatever little nigga." Mega laughed again.

"Seriously, ol' man everything good with y'all. I ain't really feeling the circles you going in about the situation."

"Me and ya mama have been through hell and back and always came back on top. There is nothing in this world that could come between the love that we have for each other and I believe that with my whole heart. You have nothing to worry about. That's mine till the grave." Mega said that last part more to himself. He knew what he had done was something serious, but he also knew that no matter what they were going to get through this, no matter what. "And I got yo ol' man nigga, I bet I take that fine ass woman you trying to lock down on the ride of her life." He winked at Kahleno.

"Pops I might have to roll yo old ass for that one." Mega laughed at his son.

"How's that going? Kahlil told me that you and Karson got into it because you called Sutton in her house. He said his mom was not happy with him at all."

Kahleno's nose flared, he hated that Karson was playing these dumb ass baby mama games. He had been with other women before, but none had been around his son and none had gotten close enough to him to be more than just a fuck. She didn't feel threatened, but now she does.

He doesn't ever remember giving her any inkling that they were ever getting back together so he was confused as to why she felt any different. The fact that she got on Kahlil about having a relationship with Sutton was making him so got damn mad.

"I'ma handle Karson's ass. She know that's one thing I don't play about and that's my son. She's doing this childish shit because somewhere in her twisted ass mind we gone be together again and that is the farthest thing from the truth."

"Ol sack stealing ass. She was gone trap you real good." Cassidy said with a smirk on his face. He thought the whole situation was funny. "You was gone be walking around with about six got damn kids and not even know it."

"Shut the fuck up Cas." Kaleno threw an apple at him that was in the bowl on the table beside where he was sitting.

Cassidy caught the apple and bit into it and smiled hard. He didn't understand why his brother was so uptight about the situation. He felt like he should have known what was up when the bitch told him she wanted another baby, he said no, and she started tripping. That's when his guard should have went up.

"So, Sutton still playing hard to get?"

"Nah, she knows that the connection is there she just want to tie up loose ends before she hops on my shit and I can respect that. I'm trying to give her the time that she needs but she taking too long."

"How you gone rush the girl? Now if she hurry up and run to you and not really over dude then yo ass gone be somewhere with a fucking murder charge."

"No faces, no cases." A smirk appeared on Kahleno's face. "Her bitch ass *fiancé* time is running out. That nigga need to pay up or give me what I want." The brothers laughed. "When she find out that he sold her to pay off his debt she's gone leave his ass anyway."

"That was the plan the entire time." Mega matched Kahleno's smirk. He liked the way his son thought.

"That's some bitch shit."

"That nigga was in my way, it was either that or kill em." He shrugged his shoulders. "But shorty mine, by any means." AD fired up a blunt and passed it to Kahleno, he normally didn't smoke but today he just wanted to chill and relax with his family.

"Oh shit, I almost forgot, we need to move Menz from the westside. That nigga fucking up big time."

"The fuck you mean you forgot, AD? How the hell you forgot?" Kahleno fussed.

"Cause that nigga high all the damn time," Cassidy chimed in.

"Shut the fuck up sometimes nigga," AD said. "Man, the little nigga Vinny called and said that nigga had the set lit. I mean muthafuckas were everywhere, he had that shit looking like a set off house party. Me and Spiff went in there and shut that shit all the way down. I hate that pussy ass nigga man, seriously." AD shook his head.

"The fuck didn't you call somebody?" Kahleno hopped up.

"Fuck I need to call you for? I handled that shit."

"The fuck you do AD, something not right with you. You kill that nigga? I don't want to have to explain that shit to Aunt Meka." Kahleno was now pacing in front of the couch he was just sitting on.

"I didn't kill em, but I beat his got damn ass, I fucked that nigga shit up to. I made him clean up everything then I made that nigga count that shit in front of me while his ass was leaking. I'm putting Vinny in his spot, find somewhere else to put his ass, somewhere the fuck away from me," AD growled and then hit the blunt again. "But that was last night. I was so stressed out I went to the strip club and got fucked up with some dark-skinned thick ass stripper."

"One of them hoe's gone give yo punk ass something one

of these days." Cassidy shook his head and AD flipped him off.

"Speaking of," Kahleno started looking around the room. He had been meeting with the family lawyer about maybe starting a restaurant and he wanted to talk to his brothers while his dad was there. "I want to start a restaurant."

"Well that shit was random," Cassidy said crossing his feet at the ankles. "How long you been thinking about this shit and who in the hell gone run a restaurant?"

"It's been in the works for a couple of months..."

"Couple months?" AD and Cassidy said at the same time.

They glared at their middle brother, he was a business man through and through and they weren't. They understood that, that's why they let him handle the business part of their operation, both legal and illegal but he always made sure to run everything by them before he went off and made decisions, until now.

Kahleno just got excited about the money possibilities, because they raise and butcher their own meat, they would see nothing but profit. It would be another way for them to wash their money. Nothing but good would come out of this so he hoped they were all on board, especially AD.

"Yeah man, I didn't want to come to y'all with it until I had all the facts. Now I do, I sat down with Kay and ran some numbers. Just let me know when y'all can come down to the office and we'll go over everything and decide like we always do." All the Maler men nodded, that put their minds at ease a little, but one question still remained unanswered.

"But who gone run a restaurant Kahleno? You can't do it, you got enough shit with the business side of shit. I can't do it because you know the farm takes up all of my time. So, who the fuck gone have time to run a restaurant?"

Everybody looked around and then their eyes fell on AD. He did his thing with making X and whatever else he did in that damn lab, but he only did that like once or twice a week depending on the demand. The rest of the time he was checking behind the niggas they had in the streets. Only thing with that is they had Spiff handling all street shit, and he was solid and loyal.

"Fuck y'all looking at me for? Y'all know good and damn well I don't like people. I don't even talk to people, why in the hell would y'all want me to run a got damn restaurant?" he grilled them drawing a chuckle from Mega.

He knew that his son was pissed off because he didn't really deal with people. AD had always been an introvert. His temper was quick, and he wouldn't hesitate to fight you or shoot you and he knew it, so he stayed to himself.

When he was younger, he almost lost his life to the system for his temper. He was playing ball with some kids his age and one of the boys elbowed AD in the head on purpose. They got to fighting and AD beat the kid so bad that he had to be hospitalized.

Mega had to pay the family one million dollars not to press charges and for the kid to say that he didn't know who beat him up. The other kids that were there were scared so they never said anything. At that moment AD knew what he was capable of and tried his best to stay to himself so that side didn't come out.

"Nigga it ain't like that, you just hire someone to manage it and you just pop in to make sure shit running right." Kahleno shrugged like it was no big deal but he of all people knew AD's struggles with his temper.

"How in the fuck I'm gone do that? You know how I feel about being in the public eye! What happens if someone says or does some shit I don't like or don't do what the fuck I say, and I mess around and shoot them...then what? Who the fuck gone get me out of that shit?" They all laughed but AD didn't see shit funny.

"Dramatic ass nigga."

"Man fuck this, I ain't doing this shit. Count me out. Y'all done stressed me out. I'm going to the strip club to get some pussy." AD stood up and snatched his keys off the table and stormed out the door making sure to slam it so hard the picture of him fell off the wall near the door.

Kahleno knew that it wouldn't be an easy task to get AD to do anything besides be back in that lab and going to the strip club. He shook his head and went to the fridge to get another beer.

"Anybody else need a brew?"

"Yeah," Mega and Cassidy said simultaneously.

Kahleno opened the refrigerator, just as his phone rang. He looked at the time and it was after ten so he didn't know who could be calling but when he read the caller ID, a smile graced his face.

"My queen, you ready to claim your throne?" Kahleno's smooth voice carried its way through the phone and into Sutton's heart. Almost deterring her from the reason she was calling but her feelings were hurt that he was gonna try and buy her, so she needed to see what the fuck he was thinking.

"Where are you?" her tone was harsh, and it took Kahleno aback.

"What's up beautiful? Are we having our first marital debate and I know nothing about it?"

"Kahleno, where are you? If you don't want to tell me where you are can you meet me at my shop?" she was pissed and the urgency in her voice let him know that her bitch ass boyfriend told her about his proposal.

"I'll shoot you the address to the farm house. It's the same place you came when we first met but a little ways down that road."

"Alright text it to me." With that she hung up. Kahleno looked at his phone and then to the wall and back to his phone. He couldn't believe that she had hung up on him, but she had. That would be addressed the minute she walked through the door. That was disrespectful in his book and he wanted her to know that.

CHAPTER FOURTEEN

You're Mine Now

Driving down the long road to get to her destination gave Sutton time to reflect on the last month of her life. Things with Trouble had been rocky for a while now, but she had faith that things would somehow turn around. Looking back, she was in love with the thought of how he used to be, even though it was never what she needed.

Her mind knew that Trouble wasn't the one for her, it was her heart she was having trouble convincing. Still, she questioned the motive behind her revelation. It wasn't until she met Kahleno did she realize just how much of a shit hole she had dug herself in with this relationship that was going nowhere. She was appreciative of Kahleno for that but now she was questioning his motives too.

Just thinking that Trouble and Kahleno was talking about passing her around like a piece of meat enraged her almost to tears. She probably could have just blocked his number and refused to see him again, somewhere in the back of her mind she didn't want that.

Sutton wanted to look the man that had crept his way into her heart in a small amount of time, in the eye and hear why he would degrade her like she was a common whore. Kahleno had shown her on more than one occasion that she was special, was all that just a façade? Sutton shook her head as she felt her anger rising.

"Lord let me be able to keep my hands to myself," she said aloud.

As she turned down the long driveway, she stared in awe at the beautiful two-story brick home. You could tell that it was an older home that had been modernized a bit, the bay windows had been replaced and landscaping from what her headlights allowed her to see was magnificent. Sutton had never seen anything like it before.

Growing up in Charlotte, NC she never knew any of this existed. They were tucked away nice and I guess that would benefit them in a way.

"Why are you sitting in the car?" Mega asked Sutton making her jump. She had been so enthralled in looking at the house that she wasn't paying any attention to her surroundings. Still holding her chest, she turned off the ignition, rolled up her window and unlocked the doors.

She took in the older version of Kahleno and he was even

more handsome than the first time she saw him. Offering up a soft smile, Sutton allowed Mega to open her door as she slid out of the car. It amazed her how comfortable she was around them.

The feeling that Mega got when he first met the light skinned beauty, magnified. She reminded him so much of Siya, his beautiful wife. He just hoped that his son was a smarter man than he was and kept his mistakes at a minimum.

"Where's your son, I got a bone to pick with him." Sutton said not easing up on the attitude. Mega threw his hands up and his grin turned into a full-fledged smile. She was the one.

"What did his bone head ass do now?"

"I can't even bring my lips to say."

"Well whatever it is, I hope the two of you can get through it. Let me walk you in," he said touching the small of her back, leading her to the house. It wasn't in a sexual way, nor was it romantic, it was more of a father leading his daughter. Sutton welcomed it.

"Pops, I knew yo old ass was taking too long out there. Why you got yo hands on my woman?" Kahleno said opening the screen down wide and coming into view.

Mega chuckled at his son trying to throw his weight around, he'd better be glad that he was madly in love with his wife because if not he'd give his son a run for his money.

"I'm not your woman." Sutton said voice full of aggravation.

"Guess you heard that." Mega said stepping around Sutton and making his way into the house. When he got to where

Kahleno was standing, he smiled at him. "You better fix it! If you let her get away, you'll regret it. I promise you." With that he disappeared into the house to call his wife like he had been doing every night to beg for her forgiveness.

"Hey beautiful." Kahleno smiled at her, he had an idea about what she was so pressed about but he wanted to hear it from her. Until she spoke her peace, he had every intention of fucking with her.

"Ohhh don't you hey beautiful me. I'm so damn pissed at you." Sutton pressed her hot pink fingernail into his chest.

He looked down at her finger and then into her eyes. Normally that would grant a physical reaction out of him and not in a good way but with her he felt a sexual energy. Unable to resist he pulled her in and pressed his lips against hers.

Sutton was caught off guard by his gesture, and as bad as she wanted to pull away, she couldn't. His presence had a hold on her that she couldn't shake. His lips felt so damn good, the way his thick tongue explored her mouth momentarily paralyzed her mind.

Kahleno's dick was so hard it was struggling against the zipper of his tailored slacks. It wanted out so bad, it wanted out to get acquainted with his new home. If Kahleno had his way he was going to make sure he got just that.

"Whoa, no wait. What the fuck?" Sutton said winded, she didn't mean to get so carried away in him but that's what happens when she gets around him. Her guard drops and any ounce of restraint that she thinks she has is gone the second their eyes connect. "What are you doing to me?" she thought she said to herself but the smirk that spread across Kahleno's face let her know that she didn't.

"It's fate baby girl, that's all there is to it. You can fight as much as you want to, but this is meant to be." Sutton's palms became moist and she rubbed them against the shorts that she had on.

"Yo—you don't know that." Kahleno leaned in causing her words to get caught in her throat.

"Yes, I do. Whenever you're around me your palms get sweaty," he reached for her hand and placed hers in his, they too were moist she looked at him with a shocked expression. "And your stomach gets to rumbling." He moved her hand to his stomach, "Then your heart starts beating out of control." Kahleno slowly slid her hand from his stomach, up his chest and over to where his heart was beating just as fast and hard as hers was. "And even though it seems crazy as fuck, I don't want it to stop."

Sutton was stuck, she couldn't even formulate the words to curse him for what he did. At that point in time none of that was relevant. She just wanted to feel him close to her, his lips against her and his body wedged between her legs. She wanted that and Kahleno was going to give it to her.

Without saying another word, he pulled her inside of the house and led the way up the stairs. Sutton didn't object and Kahleno didn't give her a chance to. Words at this point were unimportant, actions were needed to solidify the connection that they both were feeling.

When they got to the room that Kahleno use to occupy as

a child he shut the door and opened the window. The moon had a perfect view of Sutton's golden skin and it made her glow. Kahleno smiled because that's the exact way that he pictured her in his dreams.

"I don't think—"

"Don't think, feel," Kahleno said to her as he pressed his thick lips against hers and sent a volt of electricity into her body. It stopped at her pussy and her clit throbbed, so much that it was beginning to hurt. She wanted him, no, she needed him right now.

Grabbing the sides of his face Sutton deepened the kiss, her tongue painted her name in the inside of his mouth, and he enjoyed every second of it. When he felt her relax in his arms, he knew that was his green light to make her feel like the queen she was, his queen.

The deeper the kiss got the more clothes hit the ground. Taking the hem of her top Kahleno pulled it over her head showing that she was braless. Her round perky breast sat up damn near perfect and made his mouth water.

"Damn," he moaned as he took it into his mouth and lightly sucked right before he ran his tongue around the nipple then flicked it back and forth.

"Ummm." Sutton couldn't really put into words what she was feeling at the moment, but she knew that she had never felt that way before. She was sure that tonight was going to be a night that she would remember.

Moving to the other breast Kahleno worked his way out of his slacks and boxer briefs. Sutton reached around to grab his manhood and when she got it in her hand, she immediately let it go and looked down at it. Kahleno chuckled and pulled her back to him and kissed her lips.

"Don't worry baby, you'll get use to him. He's not as scary as he looks," he said against her lips. She wanted to object but she felt Kahleno's fingers dancing around her clit and she let out a moan instead. "Damn you wet, I need to taste this."

Backing her up against the bed, Kahleno slowly and gently laid her on the bed. Sutton suddenly felt shy under his gaze but the minute his hands were on her she was comfortable. He nudged her to move back.

The moon shown down on the prettiest pussy he had ever seen. She was neatly waxed and smelled clean. He couldn't wait to dive in, and he didn't. Kahleno drug his tongue from her opening up to her clit, encircling it and then bringing it into his mouth and sucking. Sutton's legs immediately began to shake.

Sutton pulled her bottom lip in between her teeth as she lightly bit down, she was trying her hardest not to scream out knowing that his dad was somewhere near. Kahleno could feel her holding back and he hated that. Silent fucking repulsed him, he wanted to know that he was making her feel good.

"It's too quiet in here." he said against her pussy and the vibrations from his words made Sutton thrust towards him inadvertently. "Oh yeah." Kahleno smirked to her gesture. "Bet!"

He dipped his head into her pussy and moved his tongue up, down, side to side, in a circle, after a while Sutton got tired of trying to keep up with what he was doing and fell victim to the euphoric state that she was headed in.

"Oh, shit Kahleno, yes! Oh god that feels good." She couldn't hold it in anymore. "Fuck yes!"

That excited Kahleno, he went in on her pussy after hearing her cry out like that. He inserted his tongue in her pussy, made it real stiff and started to work it in and out of her while applying pressure to her clit with his thumb.

Her pussy had a sweet taste to it, Kahleno was falling in love with it every minute he was down there. He was slowly becoming an addict and she was his drug of choice. Kahleno's tongue moved back to her clit and his fingers took the place of his tongue, inside her. He alternated between sucking on her clit and flicking back and forth across it while his fingers assaulted her g-spot.

Sutton's mouth hung open while she mumbled a bunch of shit that not even, she could understand. He was taking her body to heights that were unheard of. Right when she was about to cum, he would switch and do something else and it was driving her crazy. It was like he was doing it on purpose, like he knew her body that well already.

"Ssss shit Kahleno."

"Not yet," he removed his fingers and pushed her legs back a little more so that he could get better access.

"Baby please." She begged and that shit turned Kahleno on to a point that he almost couldn't contain himself. His heart was trying to beat outside of his chest and his dick was pounding even harder. He wanted inside of her so bad that it hurt but he wanted her to cum first, he needed that from her.

Dragging his thick tongue up and down her pussy really fast made Sutton throw herself in his direction. When she grabbed the back of his head and grinded her pussy in his face he sucked on her clit until he felt her legs began to shake.

"Oh God yes, yes, yes, yes, ssssssssssssss! Oh shit." Sutton came long and hard. Her eyes shut tight as Kahleno flicked across her click making her cum harder. She didn't know what he was doing to her but every nerve in her body was tingling and every limb was shaking.

Her body was jerking and doing shit that was out of her control. She didn't think she had ever experienced what she was experiencing right now. It was feeling so good to her she was afraid to open her eyes in fear that it was a dream.

Kahleno took this as the perfect time, he licked her clean from her opening to her clit causing her to shiver under his touch. He grabbed the base of his dick, climbed in the bed with her and placed his head at her opening.

She was in such bliss that she didn't even realize what was going on until he started to push himself into her. Her body was still taking her through a million and one exultant changes that she wasn't in her right mind to process the pain.

"Man, you have got to be shitting me," Kahleno said as he worked his way into her heaven. He knew that she would have good pussy but there was no way that he would have thought that it would be like this. "Fuck, girl. This has to be a got damn dream."

Sutton was thinking the same thing. She was starting to come down off of her high when the tip of his dick pressed against her spot and took her right back where she had just came from.

"Oh, shit Kahleno, baby that feels so got damn good." She moaned throwing her head back. Kahleno leaned down and crashed his lips against hers.

"That shit was sexy as fuck, say that shit again." he taunted. She opened her mouth to say it again, but nothing came out. She wrapped her hands around his waist and pulled him into her. Kahleno knew he was in trouble and he was going to have to practice the most self-control that he's ever had to in his life. "Say that shit again." he whispered in her ear making her shutter.

"Kahleno that shit feels good," she obliged.

"Ya pussy is so got damn tight and wet, you know you're mine now?" Kahleno growled in her ear. "Fuck Sut."

The way her pussy wrapped around his dick and drenched it had Kahleno in another world. He could feel his nut coming but he knew that he wasn't done, and he didn't plan on stopping anytime soon.

"Go deeper!" she egged him on, and he put her legs in the cuff of his arm and grinding into her as far as he could go. He could feel her wetness on his balls and that had him moaning out her name.

"Ssssss Sutton."

"Ummm say that shit again that was sexy." She mimicked his words from earlier. He leaned up and looked at her with a smirk on his face. He moved his hands under her back and grabbed her shoulders slightly lifting her off the bed. Leaning back on the heels of his feet he had her in the position to do whatever he wanted to do to her, and he planned to do just that.

Kahleno began fucking the shit out her, he was moving at a quick pace. You could hear their skin slapping against one another as he showed her who the fuck he was. She accepted everything that he was giving and deemed him the best she'd ever had, after only this one encounter.

"Kahleno I'm about to cum. Oh god I'm about to cum all over your dick, shit!" Sutton called out and that excited Kahleno even more.

He too was about to cum, he knew that he needed to pull out, but he couldn't, and truth be told he didn't want to. He had no intentions of pulling out of her until the sun came up. This was his new favorite place and he was going to stay there as long as he could.

"Oh fuck." He hissed and bit down on his bottom lip as he felt her pussy gush on to him. He couldn't hold it anymore as his nut traveled from his stomach into her womb. They both cried out together, as Kahleno slowed up his motions. "Got damn girl, you just don't know what you've done." He said but Sutton was on another planet, not paying attention to anything that he was saying.

Kahleno moved in and out of her at a slow pace, just to give his sensitive head a few to get back right. He never lost his stride and his dick stayed hard. It didn't take long for his body to bounce back and he grabbed both of Sutton's legs and held them straight up. She was as limp as a rag doll, but her pussy was still juiced up, that's all that mattered to him right now.

"I want you to fuck me from the back." Sutton said softly, Kahleno looked down at her and smiled. He loved a woman that knew what she wanted.

"I thought you was out." he said still moving in and out of her slowly.

"Nah, I feel damn good but I'm just getting started." She gave him a lazy grin. Sutton had the sex drive of a teenager and she loved a man who could hang with her, what she didn't know was that Kahleno had just as much stamina as she did.

"That's what the fuck I'm talking about, turn yo sexy ass over then." Sutton turned over and raised her ass in the air and arched her back perfectly. Kahleno looked down at the beautiful vision in front of him and he couldn't help but smile. "You gone be my wife!" he said more to himself as he slid into her nice and slow. This woman was about to change his life, he just hoped like hell that he was prepared for it.

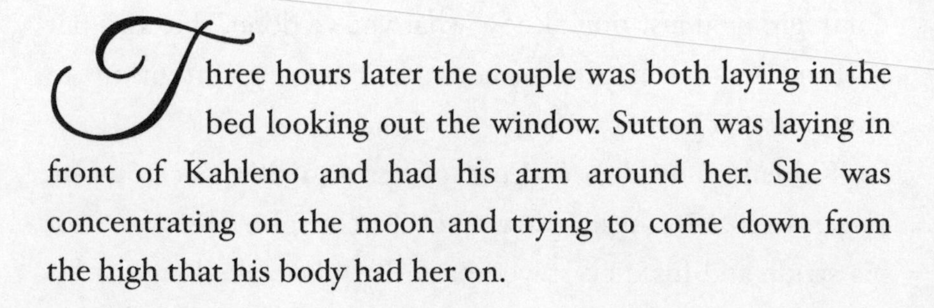

Three hours later the couple was both laying in the bed looking out the window. Sutton was laying in front of Kahleno and had his arm around her. She was concentrating on the moon and trying to come down from the high that his body had her on.

"What you thinking about beautiful?" This was the most relaxed that Kahleno had ever been since he first got with Karson. For the longest he hated her for taking these kinds of moments away from him, he was thanking Sutton for giving it back.

"Why did you offer to wipe Trouble's debt clean to have me for a weekend?" Her body tensed up in his arms as everything that she had planned to say to him came rushing back to her mind. "Do you know how that made me feel? Like I wasn't worth nothing, like I was a whore to be passed around amongst the crew. That shit hurt me because I thought what we had, whatever it is that we have was real."

"Trouble was in my way. I wanted you, from the minute I saw you. I knew that you were what I needed. I told you that, if you thought I was playing that was on you. When I want something, I'm going to get it by any means necessary." His words were firm and held power to them. "I never said that I wanted to fuck you, I said I wanted a weekend away with you. I would never treat you like a hoe, you're better than that. We are better than that."

"But can you see how that shit would make me feel?"

"I do and I hate that you felt like that and I will do everything in my power to make up for that, but I had to do what I had to do to secure my future and you Sutton are my future. It was either, he was going to tell you that bullshit or you were going to agree to it to help him. Either way, you were going to be in my presence and that was going to be the end of you and him."

"So, you just had it all figured out huh?"

"By any means necessary." Kahleno smiled even though she couldn't see him. "I'm just glad that it ended out like this because if not I was going to kill him. Hell, I still might have too."

Sutton peeked over her shoulder to see just how serious he was and there wasn't a once of humor on his face or in his tone. He glanced at her before his attention was back out the window.

"So, what now?" Sutton asked. She was so unsure of whether she was coming or going when she was in his presence and she knew that was dangerous. She could easily get lost in him and was she really ready for that right after she had just got out of a toxic relationship?

"That's on you, I know you just got out of a relationship." Kahleno stopped and then started again. "And if you ain't out you will be after today. I know you need time to get that shit out of your system and I'm willing to give you that but..."

"But?"

"Yeah but." Kahleno pulled her closer to him. "Patience is a virtue that I don't possess so you're gonna have to get over him, while getting to know me."

"I think I can do that." Sutton said just above a whisper.

Kaleno climbed back on top of her and looked her in the eyes, "Don't think shorty, you gotta know. I'm not good at sharing and I'm not good with the back and forth. You either in this or you're not." He searched her eyes for any indication that she didn't want this, and he didn't find any.

Sutton couldn't lie, she was scared shitless, on top of the fact that she had just got out of one relationship and was diving head first into another one. Swallowing hard she looked up at him.

"I'm scared," she said honestly.

"I feel you but check it, I ain't perfect, I'm telling you that now. I ain't. I'ma fuck up and you gone fuck up, but this will work. We are gonna make sure of it. Are you willing to take this ride with me?" Kahleno looked into Sutton's eyes and like usual she got lost in him.

"I'm ready." She wasn't confident in her words, but her heart wouldn't let her say anything other than what her lips spoke to him.

Kahleno smiled and once again slid into her nice and slow and they made love to the early hours of the morning.

CHAPTER FIFTEEN

Back to Business

"Hey daddy," Sutton said through the phone.

"Hey baby, why you sound so damn chipper? What's done got into you?"

"Nothing, I'm on my way to the shop and just wanted to call you and say hey. Oh, and did you check your account? I put your money back."

"I didn't ask for that money back Sutton, I did that so you can get on your feet."

"I'm on my feet dad, no worries. I got money in my account, I took Trouble off of my account and linked my personal account with my business account. I'm good."

"What changed?" Hudson was on alert because in a week's time she went from the bank calling around to get a payment to having money, paying him back, and all this extra stuff. He prayed that she wasn't taking money from a nigga.

"Nothing dad, I'm just seeing things a little clearer now." Sutton giggled.

"Don't open one door without closing and locking the other."

"The door has been shut, locked and dead bolted. But I'm not gonna stop my life because one man didn't treat me right either."

"I knew it, who is he?" Hudson prayed that she was talking about a doctor, or lawyer, a white-collar nigga but in the pit of his gut he knew that she wasn't. She knew how he felt about her being with street niggas. His worst fear is that she's gonna end up like her mother and he didn't want that for her.

Sutton hated that she had to hide so much about herself because of her past. Her dad would have gone crazy if he would have known the extent of her relationship with Trouble. She didn't tell him half the shit that went on in fear that he would act irrational, they didn't call her father Maniac for nothing.

Hudson still blamed himself for his wife's death and he has made it his life's calling to make sure that his daughter didn't end up the same way as her mother. There was only one way out of the life and that was death, not even jail can keep you out of the life.

"Daaaaddddddyyyyyyy! Let me figure things out before you step in."

"So, you keeping secrets from your old man?" Hudson asked.

No, I just know if you found out who I was with you would have a damn hissy fit without even getting to know him. Is what she wanted to say but instead she just sighed. Kahleno was a big deal in the drug game according to Pebbles, but he didn't seem that way with her and he made her feel safe.

Sutton knew what happened to her mom had so much to do with the drug game, but she just couldn't help her attraction to Kahleno. She was attracted to bad boys and she couldn't explain it and she didn't feel that she should have to.

Maybe if her father got to see how happy she was and how much substance he added to her life then maybe it wouldn't be so bad once he knew who Kahleno was. Just because something like that happened to her mom didn't necessarily mean that it would happen to her. She just wished her father knew that.

"I love you daddy and when the time is right, you'll meet him."

"You must know I won't approve." His tone was stern, and it caused Sutton to swallow hard. All she ever wanted to do was to make her father proud, she knew who she chose to date would do the total opposite. "I just want the best for you and whether you believe it or not. I'm hard on you Sutton but I would give my life to keep you living and happy. Do you know that?"

"I know daddy." Sutton was starting to feel bad about her choices that she's made but she couldn't help who her heart connected her to. Even though she felt bad there was nothing in her that wanted to end what she was building with Kahleno.

"When you got with that nigga Trouble, I told you he wasn't right, but I let you make that decision. He wasn't in the life, but I let you do what you felt you needed to do. Now look. You deserve someone that makes money the way you do, someone that works in an office."

"He does daddy." Sutton said telling have truths. Kahleno did work in an office, running his family's business but he also did other things.

"Ummmhmmmm. Well I gotta go honey, I gotta take a meeting.

"Okay daddy, I love you."

"Love you too princess."

Hudson hung up the phone and looked as his ten o'clock appointment walked in the door. He stood up and met the gentlemen with a hand shake. One he knew from his days in the streets and the other one he didn't know at all but the fact that they looked identical he figured it was his son.

"Nice to see you again, Maniac."

"It's Hudson now." Hudson gestured for the men to sit down. He had received a call inquiring about a business deal, they wanted someone to transport meat around the North Carolina area. They spoke a few times and they were here to check out his trucks and his facility.

Mega laughed at his subtleness, he knew exactly who Maniac was. They'd done business with him for many years before his wife was killed. When they heard the news, they even offered to help in finding and taking care of the problem, but he declined, he said it was personal.

"Very well, this is my son Kahleno." Kahleno nodded and then looked around at the blank walls. If he didn't know any better, he would have thought that this office didn't belong to anyone.

"No pictures on the wall."

"Nope, when you've done half of the shit, I've done you learn to never show your hand to anyone. My family is the only hand I have left, and I be damned if I make them a walking target."

Kahleno nodded his head and took in the wisdom the old man talked about. His father told him all about the infamous Maniac and he hoped to be half the man he was. He was damn sure on his way, but Maniac was definitely someone to look up to.

"Feel that." Kahleno nodded his head in understanding. "Damn sure feel that."

The three men got down to business, Hudson gave them the tour of his facility and introduced him to a few of the drivers. The Maler men were pleased, very pleased. They wanted to work with him in more than one way.

Mega knew that Maniac was out of the game, but they needed someone to transport their product as their products from the farm. The men made small talk as they made their way back in the office. Mega and Kahleno took a seat and

Hudson closed the door and walked around to the other side of the desk.

"So, what do we think gentlemen?" Hudson asked with a smile on his face. If this deal with through he would be set, he could be able to get the two new trucks that he wanted and set up a nice account for Sutton if anything should ever happen to him. Everything he did was to make sure that she was gonna be set for life and this was no different.

"Very interested, I'll get with my lawyers and let them know that we want to do business. I'll have them draw up a contract and we can go from there." Kahleno said unbuttoning the buttons on his suit jacket.

"There is something else we would like to offer you as well." Hudson narrowed his eyes and looked back and forth between the two. "You know what *else* I do..." he started but Hudson held his hand up.

"I'm out. I don't want no parts of that scene. It took one of the best things from me and I couldn't get back into that despite the money that could be involved. I just can't do it."

"You wouldn't be involved, we would have our own driver, own truck, the only thing that we would need from you was your business front. Just to make it look good." Kahleno jumped in. "We would take all the risk and you would make twenty thousand a transaction for doing nothing." The young man shrugged his shoulders like what he was saying was nothing.

"Let me think about it."

"Sounds fair," Mega said looking at his son who shrugged

again. "But we're still set for the other business though. You'll be hearing for the lawyers soon."

"Sounds good gentlemen." The men stood to leave, they all shook hands again. They turned to leave and then Mega turned around to face him.

"I would like for you to come and see what our business is about, it's based on family. I want you to see that, and just maybe it will make your...*decision* a little easier."

Hudson thought about it for a minute before agreeing, they exchanged information and then they were gone, and Hudson was left with his thoughts. He could use the money to accomplish the things that he wanted to accomplish but even dabbling in that business made him feel like he was betraying his wife. He didn't know what to do, but the opportunity was on his mind.

CHAPTER SIXTEEN

A ***Friend of Mine***

Sutton was on cloud nine, ever since the night that her and Kahleno made love everything in her world has been going perfect. She didn't think there was anything that would take her away from the bliss that she was feeling.

"Well look at you missy." Pebbles said the minute she walked in the room. She didn't remember a time when she saw Sutton so happy. She had a glow about her, and she hoped Kahleno continued to make her happy because she deserved it.

"Heeeeyyyy Pebbles!" Sutton squealed like a little school girl and the two began to laugh. The shop wasn't open yet, so it was just her and Pebbles in there. Until the door opened and Icelynn walked in. "Oh, shit girl I forgot you were coming in early."

"If you're not ready I'm good, I'm in no rush. I just come to gossip anyway." Icelynn laughed as she pulled the ponytail holder off of her long platinum blond hair. "Hold up." she said when she looked at how Sutton was walking. "You know that dick hitting right when he got them legs bowed out a little more. Ahhh shit do tell."

Sutton burst into a fit of laughter, Icelynn was so silly when she wanted to be. She was normally on the quiet side until she was around Sutton and Piper. As so lately, Icelynn had been Sutton's shoulder to lean on in her bullshit with Trouble.

"O.M.G. I have got to tell y'all what went down, so you know I told you that I was going to break it off with Trouble right. Girlllalalalalala it was a whole muthafucking shit show. So first..." Sutton started but was cut off by Piper's loud mouth.

"Hey ladies, did y'all miss me?" she yelled making her way in the door with her makeup bag. She had been MIA for the last few days, she went with Saque to do make-up for one of his cousins who was a model. Sutton was happy for her, this would be an amazing way for her to up her clientele and even possibly get her own beauty bar like she always wanted.

"Girl ain't nobody thinking about you." Pebbles waved Piper off and she smacked her lips. "Now go on and tell us what happened before this child start going on and on about this man that we don't give a damn about. You know if you give her a second, she'll take over the conversation.

"Pebbles you just jealous." Piper waved her off. "But since

you asked. Look what Saque got me she held out her wrist and moved it around so that we could all see the diamond tennis bracelet that he bought her.

“Aww that’s cute, now Sutton go ahead and tell us why you walking funny.” Icelynn said and Piper flipped her off. They shared a quick laugh before everyone gave Sutton their attention.

“Aight so I go to the restaurant to meet with him and he starts going on and on about how we can work this out and I’m like nah bro I ain’t with it. I knew going there that I was done with the whole relationship. So, we argue a little and then I tell him how I feel. This nigga gone burst out with, well I hope you don’t think that nigga love you because he tried to buy you for a measly twenty bands,” Sutton said in her best impersonation of Trouble.

“What the fuck?” They all said in unison.

“Right, I was the same way. So, he goes on to say that Kahleno offered to clear his debt if he would give him a weekend with me.” Icelynn’s hands flew to her mouth.

“Damn he wanted the pussy that bad?” Piper said giggling.

“Bitch my shit is priceless.” Sutton rolled her eyes. “So, then I asked him well were you gonna do it?”

“What that nigga say?” Icelynn asked hanging on to every word Sutton was saying.

“He didn’t say shit, put his head down, I cussed his ass out. What kind of man offers up his woman to another man like what the fuck? I knew right then that I was completely done with Trouble. He had hurt me for the last time. So, I grabbed my stuff to leave... oh shit I forgot to tell you when we first got there this bitch that worked there named CeeCee was grilling us the whole time, I asked him if he was fucking her and he got all nervous, so I was already pissed."

"Wait CeeCee, Sunny's sister?" Piper asked. Piper had been out with Sunny and her sister a time or two, so she knew how they got down.

"You knew she had a sister? I thought she only had brothers."

"No, its two of them and like four or five brother's." Piper nodded her head.

"Anyway, so I'm about to make my exit and guess who the fuck walks in calling Trouble's name?" Sutton paused for theatrics and they all looked on ready for the bomb shell she was bout to drop. "Girl Sunny, she walked in there talking about she was pregnant by Trouble and all this shit. I was about to beat her ass but then I realized what I had to lose, and she wasn't worth it. I fired her ass and told her to come get her shit. I left them there arguing with each other."

Icelynn and Pebbles both gasped and covered their mouths. Piper went to her phone and acted like she didn't hear what she said. She knew that this was gonna come out sooner or later, she was hoping it was later after she had gotten comfortable with Kahleno. Then maybe she wouldn't care that she knew about Sunny but didn't want to hurt her.

"Did you hear what I said?" Sutton asked Piper noticing her shift in demeanor.

"I'm sorry what was that? I was all in my phone, Saque

says the sweetest stuff. He just asked me when I wanted to go ring shopping." Piper cheesed trying to change the subject. Sutton gave her a look and then shook her head.

"Did you know?" Sutton knew that she partied with Sunny sometimes, but Piper was her best friend, her sister. There was no way that she would have kept something like that from her. would she? "I know that's your girl on the party scene so did you see something or hear something I should know about?"

"What does it matter, you know now. You got rid of his bitch ass and now you gotta a good man, that's why you walking all funny right?" Piper laughed but Sutton's face heated up and she bit down on her back teeth.

"You knew and didn't tell me?"

"Look Sut, that nigga was taking you through so much I didn't have the heart to come to you and tell you no shit like that. I couldn't do you like that. One night we all went out, we were all drunk and talking shit. Cee was picking at Sunny about her knew boo and was asking if it was true about what they said about him. When I asked them who they were talking about Sunny looked at me and said Trouble. That was the last time I went out with her shady ass and that's why I don't really talk to her like I used to." Piper rolled her eyes.

"But you're my fucking friend Piper. You should have told me. Got me out here looking stupid and shit and you knew all along." Hurt dripped from every word she spoke, it felt like someone was punching her in the gut as she sat here looking at Piper who didn't think she did anything wrong.

"Saque said that I should mind my business because you may not want to know no shit like that. He said that some women would rather be left in the dark."

"Saque don't know a muthafucking thing about me to even comment anything about me but you do and you know I would want to know."

"Sutton if it were you, you would do the same thing?" Piper scoffed.

"See that's the difference between me and you. A man don't have to tell me how to be a friend. I swear every time you get a nigga you change."

"Damn now you don't want me happy, let me get the fuck out of here before one of us say some shit we don't mean." Piper grabbed her bag to leave, she would just have to have her appointments come to her apartment. Saque was in the process of finding her a building anyway.

"I tell you what, since Saque know so got damn much and that's where your loyalty lies. Make sure that nigga know how to be there for you when he fuck your ass over." Sutton yelled and then disappeared to the back in her office.

She needed to get from out in front of Piper before she put hands on her friend. The love she has for Piper, the shit that she's done for Piper and the way that she turns on her every time she gets with a man, hurt Sutton more than anything that she could have known.

Normally Sutton would sweep it under the rug but not anymore, she was tired of being there for people and not getting it reciprocated. Her love for Piper was still there, no question but she just knew how to handle her.

"You good girl?" Icelynn walked in and sat in the chair in front of her. "Don't sweat the small shit." she smiled. "You just know how to handle her from now on." Sutton nodded, she was thankful for Icelynn in this moment.

CHAPTER SEVENTEEN

A ***Family Affair***

"Mom dukes, I'm so glad you're here." Cassidy wrapped his mom up in his massive hands. She hugged his neck as he lifted her from the ground.

"I'm glad to be home. Have you settled down yet, found someone to give me grandkids yet? Huh boy?" she scolded him.

"What was that pops? I'll be right there." Cassidy yelled out pretending that someone was calling him. Siya laughed at her son's silliness, she knew that Cassidy would be the last one of them to ever get married or settle down. He was too stuck in his ways, things had to go a certain way for him to be comfortable.

Siya smiled looking around the back yard at her kids, life hadn't always been easy dealing with a Maler man, but it was worth it. She couldn't picture her life with our any of them, even Mega, whom she was furious with right now.

From the way things were flowing and how light the mood was, there was no way he told them what he was supposed to tell them. There was no way. She hated to be the one to put a damper on the mood but before they got on the plane to head back to Florida, he was telling his sons the truth.

"Mama!!!" Kahleno said the minute he walked in the yard and laid eyes on his favorite lady. He was the true definition of a mama's boy and Siya welcomed it. She hugged her middle baby and smiled at the way he was dressed.

"I swear you are your father." She shook her head and kissed each cheek.

"What about me?" Mega walked up and wrapped his arms around Siya's waist, leaning down to kiss her cheek. His touch ignited so much in her, that's why when they fell out, she made him leave. She knew that if he was in her presence that she would give in and he didn't deserve her forgiveness yet, not until he made it right.

"I was talking about your clone right here." Siya smiled and it lit up the room. Kahleno couldn't help but to smile, the love that his parents had for each other was unmatched and he could only hope to feel what they feel one day. One thing he was sure about was that Sutton was going to be the one to make him feel like that.

"That's my son." Mega winked. "Just wait til you meet Sutton, it's gonna be like looking in the mirror. Just watch." Mega kissed her cheek again before he unhanded her and slipped his hands in his pocket but never created space between them.

"Where is this woman that I keep hearing so much about? You scared to give your ol' lady a crack at her." Siya winked and Kahleno chuckled.

"I don't know ma, Sutton is a firecracker. She might give you a run for your money."

"Don't get it twisted son, I'll beat her ass just to show you I can. Don't threaten me with a good time. Ain't nothing wrong with these hands." Siya said with so much class and poise that would have thought she had just said she couldn't wait to hug her.

"Damn ma chill. You can't be trying to beat up your daughter-in-law." Kahleno held his hands up in surrender. "But she's on her way, I hope like hell that Karson get here with Kahlil and then get on about her business."

"Do I need to slap her a few times? You know I will." Siya smiled and Kahleno shook his head. "Is that my baby boy?" Siya beamed as Adoreé walked in with a huge smile on his face. He was so excited to see his mother. Kahleno may have been a mama's boy but AD was the closest one to her.

"Maaaaaaa." He drug out as he pushed Kahleno out of his way to get to his mother. "Why you ain't come with this nigga?" He smirked with his daddy.

"Keep it up Adoreé, I'ma bust your ass."

"No, you ain't Mega leave him alone." Siya fussed and AD smirked. They all shook their heads because he had been that way their whole life. "I didn't come because I was giving your father enough time to tell y'all what he needed to talk to y'all about."

"What's up pops, what you got to rap to us about?" Kahleno asked.

"Maaawwwwmaaawwwww!" could be heard from miles away. Kahlil came tearing through the yard. Cassidy caught him and picked him up right before he could reach Siya.

"Nah, you ain't getting my mama. Ion know what the fuck you thought this was," Cassidy said turning Kahlil upside down by one of his legs. "What you thought you was about to come here and get all the attention, fuck that."

"I'ma fuck you up, watch," Kahlil said with ease. Siya shook her head, she was going to get on them about all that cussing they do in front of him.

"KAHLIL!" everyone in the yard yelled at the same time.

"I know, I know, I know," he said as Cassidy burst out laughing and put him right side up. He turned around and punched Cassidy in the nuts and sent him to his knees.

"I'ma fuck you up Kahlil."

"Catch me first." Kahlil laughed before he turned around and latched on to his grandma. It had been months since they saw each other. Kahlil loved his grandmother, especially when she cooked his favorite, mac-n-cheese.

"I'm gonna wash your mouth out with soap if I hear you cuss again," Siya said in Kahlil's ear and he just latched on to her neck and she picked him up. "I missed you so much, so much so I cooked your favorite!"

His eyes lit up, in his mind no one cooked mac-n-cheese

like his mawmaw. That would be all that he ate today, Siya was sure of it. Wiggling down Kahlil seemed so excited to get to someone.

"Sutton!" Kahlil yelled and took off running and latched on to Sutton.

Siya stood back and watched as the light skinned beauty picked him up and swung him around. He hugged her neck and kissed her on the cheek. She smiled and a peaceful vibe fell over the whole yard.

"Oh, how I've missed you, when are you coming back to get your hair cut?" Sutton asked and Kahlil looked at his mom and got a sad look on his face.

"He's not!" Karson came around the corner and snatched Kahlil away from Sutton. Sutton looked at her like she was crazy, if it weren't for the look that Kahlil was giving her, she would have snatched the bitch bald, but she didn't want to show out in front of him.

"Karson, what the fuck is wrong with you? You clearly done lost your fucking mind. Bit—" Kahleno started but Sutton stopped him.

"Kahleno don't do that, not in front of Kahlil. It doesn't matter what's going on, don't disrespect her in front of him. He's watching you, not her." Sutton pointed at Kahleno and then Karson who smacked her lips.

"Let's go Kahlil."

"You are not taking him anywhere, we talked about this. I don't know what your problem is but I'm not dealing with it. He's gonna be around Sutton, and there is nothing you can do about it. Now we can do this the civilized way, or we can do this the hard way Karson. If you want to do it the hard way then I can go ahead and tell you now, you lose."

"It's not right Kahleno, you were just with me the night Kahlil got sick and now you parading her around your family like she's something."

Sutton bit down on her back teeth, she was pissed because Kahleno lied to her, but she would never show another bitch her hand, so she stood there very unbothered. Kahleno could feel Sutton's vibe change, but that's because their connection was that close. No one else saw that but him. He knew he should have never fucked with her and that was his fault.

"Ma, will you take Kahlil in the house? I just want to set something straight real quick." Siya reached out for Kahlil and he took off in her direction. He hated when his parents fought, and he hated when his mom talked bad about his dad in front of him, it made him sad.

"Daughter would you like to join us in the house?" Siya stopped shy of the door and turned to ask Sutton. Karson's mouth dropped because Siya always called her by her name and requested that she not call her mom but Siya.

"Sure, I mean that's if it's okay with Kahlil." Sutton turned her head and smiled.

"Are you a clout chasing hoe? That's what my mama said," Kahlil asked innocently. He was referring to the conversation that his mom had with her friend the other night, where she called Sutton a clout chasing hoe.

"A what?" Sutton unintentionally balled her fist and her

head snapped in the direction of Karson. "I don't call you out of your name and I demand the same respect. This can get nasty, really nasty but out of respect for your son I'm gone bow out gracefully," Sutton said through gritted teeth making Mega and Siya smile. Kahleno was too busy grilling Karson. "Kahlil, sometimes grown up say things that they don't mean because things don't go their way." Kahlil nodded his head like he understood. "Do you know what that means?" Sutton asked.

"No, I just heard it."

"Well maybe you shouldn't say things if you don't know what they mean." She smiled at him.

"I think you fine as hell, I know what that means," Kahlil said, and everyone laughed except for Karson and Kahleno who was in a serious stare down. Sutton shook her head and followed Siya and Kahlil in the house.

Kahleno was trying his best to contain himself, but it was proving to be harder than he expected. He never took Karson as the messy baby mama type, but she was proving him wrong every day.

"I don't think it's right..."

"Shut the fuck up Karson, just shut the fuck up. You gone listen and you gone listen good." Kahleno closed the gap between the two of them. "Make this your last time coming out your mouth about Sutton. She ain't done shit to you but lock down the man you lost and that was your fault. That woman don't want nothing from me, she got her own business, making her own money, she got a house car and nice bank account. The fuck she chasing? Do you see how she just fixed the bullshit that you instilled in our son? You should be glad that that's the kind of woman I have around him!" Kahleno raised his voice and pointed to the door where he noticed that Siya had the window opened ear hustling. "But no, you want to act like a bitter bitch. Well let me break it down for you, yeah, I let you suck my dick, and yeah, I almost let yo sneaky ass get me again, but that shit won't happen again. There is nothing that I want from you except for you to be a good mother to our son, there is no us, there never will be. With or without Sutton in the picture I could never trust you again. So, stop doing this to yourself and move the hell on."

Tears fell rapidly down Karson's face, again she had put herself in a situation to look like a fool. This wasn't her, it wasn't who she was but her love for Kahleno was taking her out of character. She needed to find some kind of resolve and soon because this was gonna drive her crazy.

Without another word she turned on her heels and headed for her car. Kahleno watched until she disappeared around the house. Once she was gone Sutton came out the door and she looked like she was pissed. Once she got to where Kahleno was she placed her hands on her hips.

"We gone talk about the other shit, I don't care if it was before we established our..."

"Relationship," Kahleno finished her sentence.

"Okay but that's something that I should have known, especially seeing as though she wants her family and could use that as something to come between what we're building. You got to be straight with me about shit like that. Don't hide things from me. Tell me... and give me the choice to decide if I want to deal with it or not." She looked deep in his eyes and his heart shuttered. "Now," she wrapped her hands around his neck, "thank you for taking up for me and putting her in her place. If it wasn't for Kahlil, I would have put my foot in her ass." Sutton smiled and Mega laughed.

"She is your mother." He shook his head and so did Kahleno. It was true he was falling in love with someone just like his mother.

"Hey, we have another guest," Siya said rejoining everyone with their guest.

Kahleno pressed his lips against Sutton and she welcomed it. She was planning to reward him for how he handled that situation. Most men would have let it go to keep the peace, she loved how he shut it down right off the back.

"Ahhh thank you for coming Hudson," Mega said as Hudson made his way down the stairs. His attention wasn't on Mega though. He wanted to make sure that his eyes wasn't deceiving him. Mega noticed the way he was looking at Sutton. "You remember my son; this wonderful woman is..."

"Sutton?" Hudson's voice boomed.

"Dad?" Sutton's eyes stretched. This wasn't going to be good.

To Be Continued...